CONCEALING MAGIC

USA TODAY BESTSELLING AUTHOR
ALICIA RADES

Published by Crystallite Publishing.
Produced in the United States of America.
Cover design by Rebecca Frank.

To you.

*E*very supernatural being lives by one single rule: Never let a human see you as your true self. No wings. No essence. For all intents and purposes, when you're around a human, you are human.

But I wasn't human. I was a Davina—or an angel, as some stories went, though the stories were way off—and I wasn't going to let my powers go to waste. That's why I was attending the academy. It was a Davina's best chance at making a difference in a world where our essence—our magic—was otherwise kept a secret. And come hell or high water, I would make a difference.

The thick stone walls surrounding Harris Academy came into view, and already my heart was pounding in exhilaration. I leaned forward between my mom's and dad's seats, trying to take in the wonder of the structure. The wall was made of a beautiful white brick that looked like it belonged in a sacred temple. Bright sunlight reflected off the surface, making it look more beautiful and glorious than I remembered from the times we drove by it when I was a kid. It stretched two stories high and surrounded fifty acres, enclosing the small campus inside. The campus would be my home for the next two years. Its perimeter wall kept out prying eyes and allowed us to study as ourselves—wings, magic, and all. I'd had that freedom back home at Galen High School, but somehow, this felt different. It was my stepping stone toward bigger and better things.

In the distance, tall buildings reached twenty stories high. All around us, the streets bustled with traffic as a thousand other eager freshman like me flooded onto campus from all over the country. Celia, Minnesota wasn't a huge city, but it felt like it compared to Eagle Valley, the small town I grew up in. And it was *amazing*.

"Nervous, Cora?" Dad asked from the driver's seat.

"Me? Nervous?" I feigned. Of course I was nervous. But my nerves couldn't mask my excitement. I'd been waiting for this day my whole life. "You should be the ones who are nervous."

I was grateful Mom and Dad made the trip with me. Otherwise, all eyes would be on me. With them here, I doubt anyone would even notice me.

Dad pulled up behind a long line of cars at the front gate. I craned my neck, trying to catch a glimpse of the buildings inside. I could just barely make out the Academy Center straight in front of us past the parking lot. It was four stories high and made of red brick, with various peaks in its roof that reminded me of the Galen High mansion. Rising up from the center of the building was a pointed bell tower. It was like a beacon welcoming me to my new home.

"I can't wait to check out campus," I said. "I heard they just made an addition to the Activities Center and added a new rock-climbing wall. Plus, they're working on building an obstacle course for training. Doesn't that sound cool? Oh! And I want to see the Winged Fountain and check out the bar on the lower level of the dining center."

Mom turned in her seat and frowned. She wore her brown hair up, with loose tendrils framing her face. Normally, Mom was dressed in an apron and covered in flour, but today she'd worn a sleek black dress with three-quarter length sleeves and low heels, a real business-style look. "You're only eighteen. You're not going to a bar."

"I don't have to *drink*. I hear they play live music and have standup comedians come in all the time. It sounds fun, doesn't it?" I bounced a little in my seat.

Mom smiled, but it didn't reach her eyes. "You know you don't have to do this. You can always stay home and work at the restaurant."

I sighed. This was the third time Mom had said that today. And yes, I was counting. It wasn't that she didn't want me to become an emergency responder. She knew this was everything I wanted in life and more. The look in her eyes told me it was because she wasn't ready to let me go yet.

"I'll come to visit," I told her. "I promise."

Mom's eyes brightened. "We don't have any plans this weekend."

"Slow down, Ryn," Dad said with a laugh. "You're suffocating the poor girl."

Mom gaped at him, then looked back to me. "Am I suffocating you?"

"A little," I admitted, crinkling my nose.

Mom scrunched her face up at me, but she couldn't hold the expression for long. A moment later, she was smiling. She reached back and poked me playfully between the eyebrows. "What are mothers for?"

I pushed her hand away, laughing. "Why can't you be more like Grandma Gloria? Go find yourself a rich guy like Calvin and explore the world. Let me study my powers in peace."

Mom reached over and brushed her fingers through Dad's dark hair. "I'd rather have a nice man over a rich guy any day."

Dad tilted his head toward hers and gazed into her eyes. Even after twenty years of marriage, they still looked at each other like they were on their honeymoon.

I couldn't help it. I started making gagging noises from the back seat.

"Keep that up and you're grounded," Dad teased. The man had never grounded me a day in my life.

The traffic started moving again. By the time we reached the front gates, I was sitting so close to the edge of my seat that I was practically leaning over the middle console between my parents.

A campus security officer holding a tablet approached Dad's open window. "ID, please?"

Dad pulled out his driver's license and the paperwork

the school had given us with our passes onto campus. The guy glanced at the names, then stared at my parents in shock.

"James and Kathryn Marek?" he asked in disbelief.

"That's us," Dad said with a smile. He leaned an elbow against the open window, where a soft, pleasant breeze drifted into the car.

The guy opened his mouth and then closed it again, like he couldn't find the words. Then he stuck his hand out in my father's direction. "Wow, sir. It's a real pleasure."

Yep. I was a legacy. *The legacy.* Twenty-five years ago, my parents discovered that the Davina and the Aedes— angels and demons— were more powerful *together.* They were responsible for ending the age-old war between them and bringing our races to peace. It was only because of them that the academy even existed. Before I was born, Aedes and Davina tried to kill each other. Now we were allies revolutionizing the law enforcement and medical fields. Most people chalked it up to science, to medical advancements. They still had no idea angels and demons were behind it all.

The security guard quickly scrambled back toward his papers and pressed his tablet a few times, then handed the papers back to Dad. "You're all set to go. You'll want to go straight ahead into the parking lot. Your daughter can pick up her information packet and student ID from the Academy Center. Just follow everyone else; you can't miss it. Orientation starts in three hours, so you have plenty of time."

"Thank you, sir," my dad said.

"My pleasure." The guy waved to us as Dad started inching forward. Traffic was slow, so we moved at a snail's pace.

"Wow, this place is packed," I glanced toward the parking lot, which was almost full by now. Soon, people would start having to park on the streets outside campus. "Guess it's good we got here early. You know, I think I'd still benefit from my own car. What do you guys think?"

"No," my parents answered in unison.

"Come on," I complained. "This city's huge. What if I want to go shopping or something? Will you at least consider a moped? Hey, Dad, maybe I can borrow your motorcycle for the semester."

"You can take the bus. Besides, we offered to bring your bicycle," Mom pointed out.

I crinkled up my nose. "That rusty old thing?"

Mom shrugged.

"Grandma gave me some money for my birthday," I said. "Maybe I'll—"

"You can't do this! This is police brutality!" someone yelled outside the car.

I instantly cut off and sat back in my seat to get a better look out the window. Two security guards were dragging a guy out the front gate right next to our car. He looked older than me, at least mid-twenties, with blond hair and a strong jawline. If he weren't kicking and screaming like a little girl, I might've said he was cute. But there was something about him that repulsed me. There was a sense of entitlement in his perfect hair and dark blue blazer, like he thought the world should be bowing at his feet just because he'd been born.

"No ID, no entry," one of the guards told him sternly.

"You can't just refuse people entry!" he screamed.

He kicked his legs out, struggling out of their hold. Somehow, he managed to slip his arm out of his blazer sleeve and free it. He ducked out of the guard's reach, then twisted around until his other arm broke free. He sprinted back inside the wall, but he only took a few paces before a guard jumped him from behind. The two of them went flying straight into my window with a *thud*.

My heart leapt into my throat, and I jumped back, pushing across the bench seat all the way to the other side of the car. My pulse didn't slow as the guard pressed the guy's face up against the window, squishing it flat.

"How would you like to add another trespassing charge to your record, *Colt Walter*?" the guard threatened.

"Ooh, I'm so scared," Colt replied flatly.

"Yeah, yeah," the guard said. "Daddy's not going to bail you out every time."

The guard handcuffed him and pulled him away from the window. Finally, my heart rate began to slow. Then the trespasser turned his gaze inside our vehicle, and his dark brown eyes met mine. They were hooded in so much anger and resentment that it sent a chill over my skin. He couldn't look away from me soon enough. Finally, the guard dragged him around the side of the security wall, and I felt like I could breathe again.

"Sorry about that!" the second guard called to us.

Mom just waved back to him like it was no problem.

I finally sat up straight in my seat again. "What the hell was that?"

Dad took a long breath. "My guess? A curious human."

"What?" I asked in disbelief. "People actually try to sneak into the school?"

"Don't worry," Dad replied, not really answering my question. "The school is perfectly safe. If I know the founder Casey Harris well—and I do—she wouldn't accept anything less than the best. The best facilities. The best security. You name it."

Then how'd he get in? I wanted to say, but I didn't. Instead, I said, "What do you think would happen? If humans found out about us, I mean."

"I'm sure he doesn't know anything," Mom said. "If he did, the Alliance would deal with him. There are procedures for this kind of thing."

"Okay, but that doesn't answer my question."

Dad sighed and glanced at me in the rear-view mirror. "There's a reason we've kept the Davina and the Aedes a secret for so long. When you've been keeping a secret for Millennia, there's not really a good time to come out with the truth."

"Yeah, but people would know we help them, that we heal them and stuff. It's not like they would shun us, right?" I bit my lower lip.

Mom and Dad exchanged a glance, then Mom turned to look at me. "People believe what they want to believe. Sometimes, they don't want to hear the truth."

"Uh, okay…" I said, feeling like my parents were down-playing the whole thing.

I guess they had one good point. Some things were just better kept secret.

2

"Wow, this place is amazing." I couldn't take my eyes off it all.

We'd already gone through the registration process, and I had my picture taken for my student ID. Now I was strolling alongside my parents on a wide sidewalk with a thick folder in my hand and my full backpack on my shoulders, trusting them to be my eyes as I looked all over campus. Mom rolled my suitcase behind her, and Dad carried a laundry basket full of odds and ends. The Academy Center was behind us, and a wide-open courtyard stood in front of us, where groups of parents and students roamed. At least half of them had shifted into their supernatural form, displaying their white or black wings for everyone to see.

It was so strange. Back home, we were only ever allowed to have our wings out at school. I guess that was the case here, too, but the campus was so much larger than I was used to. It was like its own mini village where we didn't have to worry about being seen. We could just be ourselves.

Tall maples and oaks shaded the walkway, until we reached a sunny clearing. In the middle of a grassy courtyard, glowing white balls of essence the size of my fist whizzed through the air. Freshman laughed and dodged out of the way to avoid getting stunned by the magic in a game of essence dodgeball.

Further down the walkway in the center of campus stood a large fountain.

"Look!" I shouted, pointing. "It's the Winged Fountain. I've heard so much about it."

The Winged Fountain was a symbol of campus, much like the bell tower at our backs. The way people back in Eagle Valley talked about it, it was like its waters contained essence itself. Aunt Allie claimed it was magical—but that was only because it was where Uncle Kyle had proposed to her.

I quickened my pace, leaving my parents behind me, and rushed up to the fountain. The pool at the bottom was huge, at least twenty feet across. Three tiers of white marble rose up from the center. At the very top was a carving of open wings bigger than my own. I quickly dug into my pocket and pulled out a penny, which I'd brought along for this very occasion. I stood at the edge of the fountain with my eyes closed, clutching on to the penny like it was my very life force.

What to wish for... What to wish for...

I could wish that Kaylee was with me. My best friend from Galen High decided she had better things to do than spend the year rooming with me at the best place on the planet. Instead, she was spending the year traveling Europe on her parents' dime. Which was cool, I guess, but it wasn't Harris Academy.

I wish... I wish Harris Academy is everything I dreamed it would be.

I tossed my penny into the fountain and heard it land with a *slosh*. Smiling, I turned back toward my parents—and promptly smacked into two-hundred pounds of solid muscle. I looked up to find myself staring into a pair of dreamy blue eyes. The guy was my age, with tousled dark blond hair and the most gorgeous cheekbones. He smiled down at me. Oh, lord. He had dimples.

"S-sorry," I stammered, stepping around him.

"My bad," he said at the same time. His voice was so smooth.

He tossed a coin into the fountain, but I was already headed in the other direction. I glanced back to catch another glimpse of him and saw that he was watching me. My cheeks went beet red under his gaze, and I clutched my folder tighter to my chest.

"Who's that?" my mom asked when I reached her.

"Who?" I asked innocently, knowing exactly who she was talking about. "Oh, that guy? I don't know."

"He's cute," Mom said.

"Oh, God." I hooked my folder under my elbow and covered my ears for show. "Don't ever let me hear you say that again."

"Ew." Mom crinkled her nose. "I meant for you."

Ugh. Don't tell me she was going to start hounding me for grandchildren already.

"I'm not here to meet guys," I assured her, which my father looked more than happy to hear. "I'm just here to study."

But as my parents and I started away from the fountain toward the dorms, I couldn't help but steal a glance back at the blond cutie. I hadn't dated in over a year. A date or two wouldn't hurt anything, right?

I barely noticed the eyes on my parents and the whispers as people recognized them. I couldn't take my gaze off the architecture around campus as we walked. Everywhere I looked, I saw Harris Academy's emblem. In color, the emblem sported one black wing and one white. Where it was etched into surfaces, like the lamps lining the sidewalk, one wing popped outward and the other was carved inward.

Campus wasn't very big. There were four co-ed dorm halls, two main class buildings—the Elemental Building and the Science Building—and the Academy Center, where most of the professor's offices were, along with the administrative departments. Close to the dorms sat the dining hall and Activities Center, which boasted three full-sized gymnasiums and an Olympic-sized pool, along with a rock-climbing wall, a gym with top-of-the-line workout equipment, and outdoor tennis courts.

We arrived at Clark Hall, and I found my room on the second floor. The door was already propped open. Inside, a girl my age sat on one of the beds, and her parents stood beside her. She was petite, with dark brown hair that fell in waves to her shoulders. She wore a cute floral-printed dress with a belt around the middle. My roommate gave a sweet smile when she saw me standing in the doorway.

"Hi!" I squealed in excitement. We'd already talked online to coordinate who was bringing what, but I hadn't had a chance to get to know her yet. "You must be Laura."

I stepped into the room and held my hand out to her.

"Cora!" She shot to her feet and bounced over to me. Instead of taking my hand, she pulled me into a tight hug. I could smell the fresh scent of her shampoo, and I felt warm in her embrace.

"Cora and Laura," I heard my mom whisper to my dad. "How cute."

Laura drew away. "Oh my gosh. It's so great to meet you. This semester is going to rock."

"Damn straight," I said with a chuckle.

"Hi," Mom said kindly, reaching out a hand to Laura's parents. "I'm Ryn, and this is my husband, James."

Laura's mom took my mom's hand, but she stared agape at my parents.

Laura elbowed her in the side. "Jesus, Mom. They're just people."

She quickly composed herself. "Of course. Where are my manners? It's just such a pleasure to meet you. If it weren't for you, Sam and I never would've met. I'm Briana."

My dad set my laundry basket beside my bed and shook Sam's hand.

"What do you mean?" I asked, glancing between my new roommate's parents.

"Oh, Laura didn't tell you?" Briana asked. "I'm an Aedes, and Sam's a Davina."

My eyebrows rose involuntarily. Mixed families had become more common in the last decade, but it almost never happened in my parents' generation. Back then, there was still so much stigma. I'd never met someone my age with mixed powers.

"That's amazing," I said, turning to Laura.

She breathed a sigh of relief, like she'd been holding her breath. Had she been afraid I'd judge her?

Briana and Sam started talking to my parents, while Laura and I spoke amongst ourselves.

"So, you can perform Aedes and Davina magic?" I asked her.

Laura bit her lower lip. "Yes."

"Wow," I said. "That must make you super powerful. Can you draw your own essence to enhance your element?"

Laura shook her head. "Unfortunately, it doesn't work that way. I still need a partner."

"But you could have an Aedes or a Davina partner, right?" I asked.

The mechanics fascinated me. Davina were more powerful than Aedes. Our essence could control the elements as well as heal, but we couldn't do it without the Aedes. They were the only ones who could access another being's essence and draw it out of them. They acted as a sort of battery, charging up our essence and helping us pull more from the earth so that we could perform these amazing acts. Without them, our essence was nothing more than a party trick.

"I'm a jack of all trades," Laura said proudly. "Except air, water, and fire." She ticked each one off on her fingers and chuckled.

"So your element is earth?" I asked.

Laura began unpacking one of her suitcases into her dresser. "Yep. I do trees, grass, rocks, you name it."

I felt a little awkward standing around, so I pulled my sheets out of the laundry basket and started making the bed. "Sounds cool. Do you know what you'll major in?"

Laura wrinkled her nose. "I could go the earthquake cleanup route, but I've also thought about focusing on my Aedes side so I could work anywhere."

I fluffed my pillow on the bed. "That sounds like a good idea. My element is fire, so I'm studying to become an emergency response technician specializing in fires and burns."

"So a firefighter?" Laura asked.

"Medical firefighter, I guess," I said as I started organizing my antiques collection on my desk. I collected anything with a story—including the Davina Blade Uncle Kyle had given me that I kept in my boot at all times. "I intend to graduate top of my class."

Not only that, but I intended to win the Chancellor's Award. It was an honor given to the top performing team in each program their first semester. It opened doors for advanced classes and future job opportunities. And it was mine.

"I'm sure you'll hit the top. You sound pretty determined." Laura finished with her clothes and turned to the large suitcase on her bed. When she opened it, I was shocked to see it was filled entirely with shoes. Heels, boots, flats, sneakers, you name it. There were shoes for every occasion.

My eyebrows shot up. "Whoa."

She laughed. "First thing you need to know about me, I *love* shoes. What do you think of these?"

She twisted her foot to display a pair of fashionable black flats with faux straps that crisscrossed near the toes.

"Cute," I said honestly.

"Second thing you should know about me, I'm a California girl and absolutely *terrified* of your winters." Laura laughed.

"Look on the bright side. The snow's a good excuse to go shopping for a new pair of boots," I pointed out.

Laura beamed. "You totally get me. I think we're going to get along well."

"I hope so," I said.

An hour later, we'd finished unpacking and had gotten lunch at the dining hall with our parents, and one thing was very clear. Laura and I were already getting along great. She was smart, determined, and had graduated top of her high school class like I had. She'd make an equally good study partner as she would a friend. Kaylee would've liked her, too.

On our way to the Academy Center from the dining hall, I caught sight of a girl with a dark pixie cut and legs that went for miles standing in the grassy courtyard. Her white wings were on display, and she was surrounded by people, both Aedes and Davina alike. They all watched in awe as she manipulated fire in her hand, twisting it into a mini tornado and then shaping her flames into the shape of a dragon. She directed her essence so it looked like the dragon was flying. It flew straight toward a guy's face but fizzled out before it hit him. He ducked, then clapped when he realized he wasn't in any danger.

The girl doubled over in laughter, and I finally got a good look at the guy she was laughing at. He was the blond cutie from earlier, the one with the dimples. And he was *laughing* with the show-off.

I couldn't explain the pang of jealousy that hit me just then. She must've been in the four-year program—and a senior. I couldn't manipulate my element like that.

I hadn't realized I'd stopped to watch them until Laura stepped up beside me. "Um... it looks like you might have competition."

I scoffed. "Competition? No way. She can't be in our class."

Laura frowned. "I think she is. I saw her at registration."

My breath grew hot. The blond cutie composed himself, and he caught my eye across the grass. My stomach flipped in my abdomen. He held my gaze a few seconds longer, then turned back to the Davina girl in front of him. His eyes sparkled when he looked at her.

"I guess you're right," I said to Laura. "I do have some competition."

3

I shook off the encounter in the courtyard as we entered the auditorium for orientation. I gazed around in wonder. It was even more beautiful than I'd imagined. The room was bathed in dark wooden tones and soft lighting. A high ceiling stretched up two stories, and there was a balcony with extra seating high above us. Beautiful designs were carved into the balcony banister. Matching ornate carvings outlined the large stage at the front and were brushed in golden paint. I loved it.

Laura leaned over to me as we sat down. "Rumor has it, there's a stone from the site of the Malum portal buried beneath stage."

"It's true," I told her, sharing in her enthusiasm. "Casey Harris said so in an interview."

Laura and I continued to speak in hushed whispers until the auditorium filled and the lights dimmed. The room slowly quieted until it went completely silent. The only sound came from the click of heels across the stage as a blonde woman my parents' age came to stand behind the podium.

Laura straightened in her chair. "Oh my God," she hissed under her breath. "It's her. It's Chancellor Harris."

Chancellor Harris raised her arms in a welcoming gesture. "Welcome, First Years, to Harris Academy."

Applause filled the auditorium. Laura and I screeched beside each other in excitement.

Chancellor Harris beamed behind the microphone until the applause died down. "At Harris Academy, we strive to prepare our students for a better tomorrow in every way possible. Our history is long rooted in the segregation of our differences. Even before the creation of man, the Divinities and Sanctities separated themselves."

We all knew the stories. My dad had been telling me about them since I was a kid. I didn't have to listen to follow along.

Before humankind ever walked the earth, the earth belonged to the gods. The higher gods, the Divinities, began to have children, who became the Davina. They created a new realm, a paradise, called Vehena, which they gifted to their children. They forbade the lesser gods, the Sanctities, from producing children, because they didn't want the power of the gods diluted. But the Sanctities went behind their backs anyway and birthed a race called the Aedes.

When the Divinities learned of their children, they took away the Aedes' immortality and marked them with darkness. They banished them to a dark realm called Malum.

But the connection between the realms was unstable, and the Aedes returned.

To punish the Sanctities for going against their wishes, the Divinities cast another curse, one that would prevent the Aedes from interacting with their parents or the earthly realm. They could only walk the earth as ghosts.

This sparked the Great War between the Sanctities and Divinities, and they eventually killed each other until there were no gods left. To show the Aedes they were nothing like their forefathers, the Davina brought life out of what remained of the Sanctities' ashes. This was the beginning of humans. This new race did not have the gods' powers, and like the Sanctities, they could not see, hear, or touch the Aedes.

At this time, the Originals—the first generation of Davina—realized that the realms were tearing each other apart. They pushed the Aedes back to Malum and sealed off the realm. By the time the last sixteen Originals made it to the portal to Vehena, they found that their realm was already on the brink of collapse. And so they had to say goodbye to their home and seal the portal for good. Vehena died.

Meanwhile, a few Aedes had managed to stay behind. As they and their children roamed a realm they could not interact with, the only way for them to grow and stay alive was to feed off the energy of humans, sucking their essence and life energy away from them in order to survive. But at the time, the Davina didn't understand their true motives, and they were at war for thousands of years.

Twenty-five years ago, everything changed. Malum

collided with earth, forming a portal that had the potential to destroy our realm. My parents teamed up with the Aedes and found a way to seal off the portal before both realms were destroyed. When Malum fell, so did the curse keeping the Aedes from interacting with the earth. The Alliance was formed to facilitate peace among the three races—Davina, Aedes, and human.

Davina in government helped the Aedes assimilate into society, granting them citizenship and other necessities to give them a home on earth. It was because of my parents that we discovered the Davina and the Aedes are stronger together, that the Aedes can help us unlock the powers of the gods, including earth-creating powers like fire, water, earth, and air.

But there was one more power that wasn't discovered until months later—healing. The government—who were the only humans who knew about us—wanted to study this power and turn us into soldiers, but we refused. They knew a war would break out if they forced us—a war they wouldn't win—so they made a compromise.

We agreed to serve in the medical field and became doctors and emergency responders. Everyone thinks medicine has changed because of recent medical advancements, but that's not true. It's because of the Aedes and Davina. The Alliance thought it was best to keep our races a secret due to fear of mass panic on both sides. Casey Harris started the academy, and we've been learning how to heal ever since.

No one outside our community knows the stories of the gods anymore—not the ones that actually existed, anyway. And that whole angels and demons stuff? So not us, but we were where the stories came from. I mean, humans with the wings of a giant eagle? How much more specific can you get? No, we weren't angels or demons, but we were still pretty badass.

Chancellor Harris told a condensed version of the story, then concluded with, "And that is why here at Harris Academy, we embrace our differences. Because our differences are what make us stronger. We stand together as one."

"We stand together as one." The crowd repeated the academy's motto.

Chancellor Harris waved to the crowd, then exited the stage. Another man came to the podium after her. He looked the same age, with black hair and a thick beard.

"Let's have another round of applause for my wife," the man said.

I inhaled a sharp breath and leaned over to Laura. "That's her husband, Kane Harris! Did you know they were the first Davina-Aedes couple to get married?"

Laura beamed as she clapped wildly. "I know! Did *you* know that he took her name because he admired her so much and thought she deserved all the recognition?"

I sighed. "Swoon. You know he teaches advanced-level Aedes Essence? Maybe you'll have a class with him."

"I hope so," she said. "He's a hottie."

I giggled. "Careful. He's married."

She shrugged. "What? I can't at least *look*?"

Kane went on to give us the rundown of campus, safety regulations, and more. He warned us of protestors outside campus but assured us that we were safe and just had to steer clear of them. When he finished, we were given fifteen minutes until we had to be outside in the courtyard with the rest of our class for full campus tours and icebreaker games.

"I guess it's time for us to go," Mom said in a sad tone as we stood outside the auditorium in the wide hallway.

"I'm gonna miss you guys," I said. At the same time, I was excited to be on my own.

"You call us anytime," Dad told me. He pulled me into a hug, and I squeezed him back.

Mom looked like she was about to cry when she embraced me. "You have lots of fun. Study hard."

I chuckled as she drew away. "You know me. You don't have to worry."

"I know," she said. "But I'm your mom. It's what I do."

"I love you guys," I told them honestly.

Far too soon, they were gone, and I was being ushered outside to the courtyard. Laura had said goodbye to her parents as well and stood beside me. We were told to find the group leaders with our color of lanyard that we'd gotten at registration.

I looked to Laura. She wore a yellow lanyard, while I wore a dark purple one. "Dang it, we're not on the same team."

She frowned. "I guess we'll meet back at the Winged Fountain?"

My shoulders fell. "Yeah, I'll see you."

She hurried off to a group of yellow lanyards, while I continued to search the courtyard for my group. I passed by at least a dozen groups before I finally saw a guy a few years older than me standing on the edge of the fountain. He had dark hair and a shadow of a beard lining his jaw.

"Purple group!" he shouted out into the crowd, with his hands cupped around his mouth. "This way to the purple group!"

I hurried over to them, but I stopped dead when I saw Blond Cutie standing in the center of the group. He had his arms crossed and was glancing around, like he didn't know anyone else. Good. I wouldn't be the only one.

"Okay, how many people do we have?" our group leader said, counting our group members. He mumbled numbers under his breath, then spoke out loud. "Fifteen. Perfect."

He jumped down from the edge of the fountain, then grabbed a clipboard and a hula-hoop that had been sitting at his feet. He twirled it around his arm a few times, then looped it over his shoulder.

"Hello, purple team!" he said enthusiastically. "I'm Kumar, and I'll be your team leader for the day."

A girl near the front raised her hand.

"Yes?" Kumar said.

"What's the hula-hoop for?" she asked.

He winked at her. "I'll get to that. Any other questions?" He glanced around, but our team stayed quiet. "No questions? Great. So, we'll be starting with some ice breakers, then moving on to our campus tour."

I noticed Laura's team was already headed off toward the Science Building. It looked like her group was starting with the tour.

"Why don't we all take a seat in the grass?" Kumar suggested.

We formed a circle facing each other. I was directly opposite from Blond Cutie. He caught me looking at him once, and I quickly turned my gaze away, blushing.

"Let's all go around and say our name, ability, and one interesting thing about ourselves," Kumar suggested. "I'll start. I'm Kumar Combs, and I'm a fourth-year Aedes majoring in surgical studies. An interesting thing about me is that I spent last summer studying abroad in India."

He looked to the girl next to him, and she dove into her introduction. My mind was racing with what I would use as my interesting fact that I barely heard what everyone else had said. When it got to Blond Cutie, though, I immediately took interest.

"I'm, uh, Kellan Greene," he said in that smooth voice. "I'm an Aedes majoring in emergency response."

My program, I thought. *Maybe we'll be teamed up.*

"An interesting thing about me..." Kellan hesitated. "My father was Ronan Greene."

Ronan Greene! So Kellan was a bit of a legacy himself. His father was a member of the Alliance. He'd been instrumental in helping the Alliance understand the Davina's healing powers and how the Aedes could help refine them.

Introductions continued around the circle before I could really process what Kellan had just said. Eventually, it reached me.

"I'm Cora Marek," I said with a smile. "I'm a Davina majoring in emergency response with an emphasis on firefighting. An interesting fact about me is that my parents are Ryn and James Marek."

Gasps traveled around the group. Kumar leaned forward in interest. "You're kidding. Your parents closed the portal to Malum!"

I beamed. "I know."

"Your parents broke the Aedes' curse!" a girl across from me exclaimed.

"Yep. Davina power, right?" I chuckled and threw a fist up into the air.

All eyes were on me, and everyone looked amazed—everyone except Kellan. When I stole a glance at him, the look in his eyes was cold. What the hell? He could brag about his legacy status, but I couldn't? It felt like a stab to the gut, and I didn't even know the guy yet.

I barely heard the last few introductions. I was still stealing glances at Kellan, trying to figure this guy out.

"Okay," Kumar said, standing. "Let's move on to a little team-building exercise."

He set his clipboard in the grass and held his hula-hoop out in front of him. He kept it at chest level and parallel to the ground. "We call this the Floating Hoop. You'll stand in a circle and each place an index finger straight out. The hoop will rest on top of all your fingers. The object is for your team to lower the hoop to the ground without anyone losing contact with it. You lose contact, and your team has to start over again. Only your index finger can touch the hoop, and you must keep your finger straight. No 'hooking' allowed."

Kumar demonstrated by wrapping a finger around the hoop. "Easy enough, right?"

I smirked. This was going to be simple.

We formed a close circle, so tight that I had to turn my shoulders to squeeze in.

"Fingers out," Kumar instructed. He placed the hula-hoop in the center of our circle. "And go!"

Before I could even think about lowering the hoop to the ground, it started to rise, like someone was pulling on it with a string. I lifted my finger to keep contact with it, but it just kept going up and up and up…

"What the hell?" the girl beside me asked in disbelief, the same time two people from the other side of the circle remarked on the strange phenomenon.

"Who's doing that?" I demanded.

The hoop reached so high that I had to stand on my toes to try to keep contact. It floated up until I couldn't touch it anymore. Several of us lost contact at once.

Kumar stepped in and took the hoop. "Looks like a few of you lost contact. You'll have to start over."

He held it at chest level again, and we all stuck our fingers out to touch the bottom of it.

"And go," Kumar said as he stepped back.

Again, the hoop began to rise, and I had to raise my finger to avoid losing contact.

"Someone's using their air power to make it float," I accused. "It's not funny."

Kumar chuckled. "I assure you, no one's using their air power. You must all work together."

I gritted my teeth. Was this some sort of joke?

Several people started talking at once, all trying to throw theories around for what might work.

"Everyone just stay still," the guy on my right said when we resituated the hoop back at our chests again.

We all tried not to move, but the hoop started floating again.

"Who's doing that?" I asked, but so many people were talking that I didn't think anyone heard me.

Then Kellan's voice came across the circle. "Blaming each other isn't going to help."

I caught his eye, and I knew the statement was directed at me.

"This exercise is about teamwork," Kellan said confidently. When he spoke, the whole team listened. "We need to trust each other if this is going to work."

We started over again, but no matter what kind of pep talk Kellan gave the team, we couldn't manage to work together. When people tried to keep their fingers steady, others pushed up on the hoop to keep contact, and we had to start all over again. It was clear from the onset: Nobody trusted each other to get this task done.

"Guys, we have to move together," I said above the other chatter. I was getting more frustrated with each passing second. No one was listening to each other. I didn't even think they were listening to me.

"Let's forget about keeping contact with the hoop for a second," Kellan said. Of course, the group quieted to listen to *him*. "If we fail, we can start over. Let's start with keeping our fingers steady. Don't worry about the hoop moving. Consider it a sacrifice for the team."

Everyone stilled as we set the hoop back in place. I tried not to move, and it was starting to work. The hoop wasn't floating.

"Okay, good," Kellan said. "Now everyone start to lower together. Ready?"

I could feel the hoop start to rise off my finger. Panicked, I followed it with my finger, and it started to rise again.

Kellan caught the look on my face, and his eyebrows knitted together. It was like he thought *I* was the problem. He held my gaze for a second longer. Whatever fluttering feeling I'd felt before when I'd caught his eye was gone. My guts started to feel heavy in my stomach.

I glanced around just to break his gaze and noticed all the other teams that had started on the courtyard were gone. They must've already finished their challenge.

We started over… *again.* And just like all the times before, the hoop began to rise.

"Everyone needs to stop lifting the hoop," I said.

Kellan was quick to shoot back at me. "I just watched *you* lift the hoop. Maybe focus a little more on yourself and a little less on what everyone else is doing."

The whole group went silent as Kellan and I held each other's gazes. I was starting to realize he was a serious jackass.

"Okay," Kumar said quickly, pulling our attention away from each other. "It looks like it's time to start our tour."

Our group stepped back, and Kumar took the hoop. "This is something you might want to try another time. If there's one thing you need to learn while here at Harris Academy, it's how to work well with others."

Kumar's eyes darted between Kellan and me.

"Let's get going." Kumar started leading us toward the Science Building.

I crossed my arms and followed behind, feeling absolutely let down that we hadn't completed the challenge.

"That was way harder than I thought," the girl beside me said.

"It was impossible," I muttered back.

An hour passed before we finished our tour. When I returned to the courtyard, I found Laura sitting on the edge of the Winged Fountain.

"How'd your tour go?" she asked as she stood and fell into step beside me.

"The tour was amazing. I love campus. But the team-building exercise… Not so much," I admitted.

"Oh, really? I thought it was fun," she said.

I frowned. "My team failed. I got that cute guy's name, though. Kellan Greene. But now…" I scrunched up my nose.

"What?" she prodded.

"I don't know, he seemed kind of arrogant," I told her. "And rude."

Laura shrugged. "There are plenty of other guys. Oh, by the way, that girl from earlier—the one with the pixie cut—she was in my group. Turns out she *is* a freshman. Her name's Celina Dyer. She's actually kind of cool."

"Oh," I said dryly, remembering the display she'd put on earlier.

"You can meet her later," Laura said enthusiastically as we entered our dorm hall. "She lives in our dorm."

We were passing by the rec room when I heard my name. I grabbed Laura's elbow and stopped dead in the hall. We paused to listen.

"You met Cora Marek?" a girl said. "She's supposed to be really good, right? Like her parents."

A guy scoffed. I peeked around the corner to see Celina twisting a piece of chalk around the end of a pool cue. She was talking to Kellan, who was arranging the balls on the table.

"I haven't seen her essence yet," he said, "but…"

"But what?" Celina pressed.

Kellan shrugged. "After our team-building exercise earlier, I'm not sure she has what it takes for the academy."

My fists clenched at my sides. Who did this guy think he was? He didn't even know me!

"If she's anything like that in class," he said, "she's not going to pass."

What a prick! I'd graduated top of my class at Galen High. I was a damn good Davina.

Gonna give me shit, Kellan Greene? Fine. Two can play at that game.

4

Classes started two days later, on Monday. Laura and I woke early for our Art of Healing I class. Her heels clicked against the tile as we headed down the hall of the Essence Building and to our lecture hall. We both had our wings on full display. Mine were all white, with hints of blue and purple that shone in the light at different angles.

Laura's were much cooler. Her feathers were white at the top of her wings, but the further down they went, the more they gradually turned black, creating a seamless gradient. The white feathers at the top shone sky blue in the light, and the black ones at the bottom shimmered a midnight blue. It was gorgeous.

"This is weird," Laura said, clutching her messenger bag to her chest as we walked down the hall. A few people took notice to her unusual wings, but most didn't seem to care.

"What's weird?" I asked curiously.

"Having my wings out," she admitted. "I don't usually do this. People stare."

I glanced up and down the hall to the passing students, who also had their wings out. There was an even mix of students with black wings and white wings, but no one had both like Laura. I loved that hers made her unique.

"No one's staring," I assured her. "Remember what Chancellor Harris said at orientation? Here at Harris Academy, we embrace our differences. Own it, girl."

Laura offered a shy smile. "You're right. I shouldn't worry."

"Your shoes are cute, by the way," I told her, glancing down at the four-inch blue heels.

"I know, right?" She stopped outside the classroom door and twisted her ankle at various angles to show them off.

"They match your dress perfectly," I said.

"Thank you," she replied in a chipper tone.

She curtsied for show, then we entered the room. The lecture hall was set up like a movie theater, with endless rows of chairs that descended into the room. Long tables stretched out along each row, and there was a large desk and projector screen at the front of the room.

The class was already buzzing with conversation as other freshman filed into the room. I noticed Kellan and Celina at the front, chatting with each other. Kellan's dark wings shimmered green, while Celina's White wings had a red tint to them.

Laura and I claimed seats in the middle of the room.

Since the academy was built for supernaturals, we didn't have to put our wings away. There was enough room on either side of us to spread our wings out without disturbing the students seated behind us. I pulled out my laptop to take notes on.

There were four words displayed on the projector at the front of the room: body, life force, consciousness, and essence. They were the four energies that make up a person—basic information all supernaturals knew from a young age. Your body was your physical self, and your life energy was the energy that kept you alive. Consciousness referred to the energy of your thought processes.

And then there was essence—your soul energy that was stored inside the earth. Everyone had it. It was just that Aedes and Davina could access it physically when humans couldn't. But we could only access so much at a time. Because of Aedes' unique ability to borrow essence from another being, they could help Davina access more—and in exchange, they got physically stronger and healthier, too. It was easier for them to borrow essence from another being than to pull it from the earth. Which meant we needed each other.

All four energies were interconnected to create balance within an individual. When life force is severed, essence energy returns to the earth to be used by later generations. It was the only thing that survived after death.

I typed the words into my computer, even though I knew them by heart.

Moments later, our professor strolled into the classroom from a door at the front. She seemed young but was probably in her forties, with tight brown curls and a friendly smile. She wore an olive-green turtleneck that had slits in the back for her white wings.

She adjusted the microphone clipped to her shirt, then looked out at all hundred of our faces. "Hello, and welcome to the Art of Healing I. I'm Professor Kovski. I'll be co-teaching this class with Professor Sanders, whom you'll meet during your lab hours. Shall we get started?"

Professor Kovski clicked a button, and the screen zoomed in on the word *essence*, where her notes were outlined on the screen. "We all know the basics behind essence energy. Alone, you are virtually powerless, apart from stunning your classmates in a game of essence dodgeball." She chuckled. "But when the Aedes and Davina team up, we are capable of so much more."

She paced at the front of the room. "You've all experienced this in high school. An Aedes member draws essence from their Davina partner to open their essence channel wider. These effects last up to three days if the team forges a strong bond, but they wane when the team is separated. We all know that any Davina and Aedes team is capable of manipulating the elements."

She clicked another button, and the screen switched to a slide highlighting the power of healing. I hurried to copy down her notes.

Professor Kovski continued. "The concept is the same with healing, but you can't do it with just anyone. Healing power is so advanced that it takes specific teams to heal. The connection between a healing team must be so strong that it creates the strongest channel to essence energy. With a strong enough connection, you can even perform channeling, a very advanced healing technique."

I barely wrote down the word *channeling* before she continued.

"Because it takes a special connection to perform healing magic, we will be testing you to see who you will work best with," Professor Kovski explained. "These pairing tests will begin next week, after we've covered healing theory."

Whispers started to spread around the room. I heard one girl a few chairs down from me whisper to her friend that this was going to be easy and they were going to be paired up for sure. Another guy got a horrified look on his face and glanced around the room, like he feared he was never going to be paired up.

"Do you want to be paired with an Aedes or Davina?" I asked Laura in a low whisper.

She shrugged. "Whoever I work best with, I guess. I don't care which type of magic I'm doing as long as my team is healing."

I smiled. "I hope we're paired up."

Our professor waited for the room to quiet, then said, "Now, don't worry if you aren't teamed up right away. It sometimes takes weeks for assignments to fill. That said, let's get started on healing theory."

She changed the slide, and a diagram showing the flow of essence from one being to another came up on screen. "When healing, essence flows in two directions. The first is from the earth, through the Davina, and to the Aedes partner. This expands the channel so that the Davina member can access enough energy to direct the flow of essence into the injured party."

I scrambled to write down every word she said, but she spoke so fast that I couldn't get it all down. It became clear very quickly that I was going to have to pick and choose which points to take notes on.

Professor Kovski continued. "When healing, a Davina will have to visualize their essence differently than when they perform elemental magic. Elemental magic is forged on strong emotions, while healing magic requires a sense of calmness and trust between you and your partner."

She continued the lecture, covering techniques behind accessing your healing power. An hour passed before the lecture finished. Laura and I followed the rest of the class out of the room.

"What class do you have next?" she asked.

"I have an hour until Introduction to Firefighting," I told her.

She frowned. "I have Aedes Essence in an hour. Do you want to grab some breakfast before then?"

"Sure," I said, and we started toward the dining hall. "That lecture was pretty cool. I had no idea healing was so involved. I thought it was just like elemental magic, but with a special partner."

"Are you nervous?" she asked. "About the tests next week and getting your partner assignment?"

"No," I told her honestly. "I'm sure whoever they find for me will be a great fit."

Laura bit her lower lip. "I've heard that some people

never get paired up. Like, they just don't have it in them to heal or something."

My stomach sank. "Don't tell me that."

She chuckled. "Why not?"

"Because *now* I'm worried," I admitted.

I'd find someone to heal with… wouldn't I?

5

The following week of testing arrived, and I was more excited than ever. Laura and I sat beside each other in our Art of Healing lab. This classroom was different than the lecture hall and had fewer students. Each table sat two people. I noticed Celina and Kellan in the back beside each other. I already knew that if they ended up together, they'd be top contenders for the best team.

Professor Kovski and Professor Sanders entered the room wearing lab coats. Professor Sanders was an older guy of at least sixty, with black wings and salt and pepper hair. He pushed a cart into the room, which had surgical trays on top.

"Oh my God," I whispered to Laura. "Are those *rats* on that cart?"

She craned her neck to get a better look. "I suppose we need *something* to practice healing on."

"Welcome!" Professor Kovski said from the front of the room. "Who's excited to start healing?"

Most of us responded with enthusiastic cheers. I couldn't believe I might actually heal something today.

"Professor Sanders is going to go around the room and hand out your rats," Kovski explained. "They are each under anesthesia. Please don't touch them until you're instructed to. Now, these rats have just come from the physiology department, where upper-class students have just performed spays on them. The incision sites have been stitched up, but it will be your job to heal the wound. Keep in mind that we are only performing a surface-level healing. You are not ready to try healing internal wounds yet. We will be rotating partners, so don't worry if you don't get it right away. Also be aware that just because you complete the task does not mean you'll be paired up with that person. Assignments won't start until at least the end of the week, so just relax and do your best."

After we received our rats, our professors stood in front of the room to demonstrate healing their own rat. They had a camera set up above their workstation, which projected onto a large screen.

Professor Sanders placed a hand on Professor Kovski's shoulder to draw her essence into himself. We couldn't see it happening, but it was obvious by the way Sanders's skin seemed to brighten with color and his eyes looked less tired.

Kovski explained everything as they performed the procedure. "Since the animal is so small, I will place only two fingers over the wound. As I feel my essence channel widen, I will direct my powers into the wound. Now, focus only on the incision site. If you try to heal the rat as a whole, you may overwhelm its body and unbalance its four energies. This can cause it to go into cardiac arrest."

We'd learned all about it during her lectures earlier that week, so all of this was just a reminder.

The ends of Professor Kovski's fingers glowed a bright white. When she drew her fingers away, the incision site was completely healed. The class broke out into a round of applause.

Kovski turned toward the class. "You may begin."

My heart pounded nervously as I stood over the rat. I reached a finger outward, but pulled back at the last second.

"What's wrong?" Laura asked.

I shrugged, but inside, I was screaming. I had to make this work. "I don't know the best angle to place my fingers."

Professor Sanders heard me and walked over to our table. "Don't worry so much," he encouraged. "Focus on your essence, and the rest will come naturally."

I nodded. "Okay, I think I'm ready to give it a shot."

Laura reached out and placed a hand on my shoulder. Tingles spread through my body as I felt her pulling my essence into herself. My magic became more and more intense the more she drew from me and the wider my channel opened.

I placed two fingers to the incision site and guided my essence down my arm and to the tips of my fingers. I expected my hand to glow like Professor Kovski's had, but nothing happened. My essence stopped at the ends of my fingers, like there was a wall blocking me from sending it toward the rat.

I pushed against that wall, guiding more and more essence toward it. My essence broke through in a single burst, and flames at least six inches long shot out of my fingers. I gasped and drew back instantly to avoid burning the rat, but I'd already singed some of its hair off. Several other people turned to look at me, but I was relieved to see they all looked like they were struggling as well.

"I-I'm sorry," I stammered, looking over to Professor Sanders.

"It's okay," he said gently. "This isn't the first time it's happened, and it won't be the last. Just relax and try again."

"You've got this," Laura said encouragingly.

"Okay," I replied with a sigh.

I placed my hands on the rat again. This time when I hit that wall, I tried not to push too much essence all at once. Instead, I waited for it to flow on its own, but it never did.

"We did it!" Celina exclaimed from the back of the room.

Kellan and her exchanged a high-five. I couldn't help the scowl that crossed my face. How'd she manage it on her first try?

Several people stopped to watch as Professor Kovski and Professor Sanders went over to inspect their work. Kovski placed a hand over the rat's abdomen and closed her eyes. Her entire hand glowed a soft white, but not as much as when she'd been healing the rat earlier. It looked as if she was using her power to inspect its body for internal injuries, rather than healing it.

Kovski sighed and opened her eyes. "You've done a

great job of healing the incision site, but unfortunately, you overdid it. Its internal organs have suffered some damage."

Celina gaped at her, and Kellan dropped his shoulders. The two looked devastated.

"No," Celina said quickly, looking over the rat. "No, that can't be right."

"Don't worry," Kovski told her. "The damage is reversible. We'll heal the rat."

"But I did it," Celina snapped. "I healed it. How could I have hurt it?"

Laura and I exchanged a glance. It felt like we shouldn't be listening in, but everyone could hear her. There was no looking away.

"It's very common," Sanders assured Celina. "But I think it's time we rotate partners."

I frowned and turned back to Laura. "I'm sorry it didn't work."

"It's okay," she said hopefully. "There are a lot of other tests this week, so we can still be paired up."

Laura waved as she headed off to the next table. Another Aedes came up beside me, and I tried to work with him to heal, but I could already feel that it wasn't going to work. He was a complete stranger, and it felt awkward when he placed his hand on my shoulder to draw my essence. I could barely feel enough energy to conjure a fireball.

Two other teams made headway on our first rotation, but neither of them had healed the incision completely.

"It's a good start," Professor Kovski had told them.

I went through three other partners as class went on,

and my rat wasn't any closer to being healed. A girl named Shaylene approached on our next rotation. She was pretty, with pale skin and dark curls. I thought I felt something with her. I'd gotten my fingers to glow, but the incision hadn't healed.

"Well, it was worth a shot," Shaylene said as she moved on to the next table. "It was nice to meet you."

"You too," I said with a smile.

My smile instantly faded when I saw who came up beside me next. *Kellan.*

He had a smirk on his face, like he thought this was going to be an interesting experiment.

Well, this is going to be a total bust, I thought. He already made it clear he didn't like me. There was zero trust here.

"What's wrong?" he asked, noticing my fallen face.

"Nothing," I lied.

"Are you ready?" His voice was kind, like he hadn't said those things about me in the rec room.

"Yeah, let's do this," I said without a hint of enthusiasm.

Kellan reached out for my shoulder, and I swore I felt tingles spread across my skin before he even touched me. His hand was warm, but everything else about him was unexpected. Essence whipped through me, and my whole body came alive with energy. It sizzled down to my toes, then back up to my head again. It felt so powerful that I wondered if anyone else could see it. With the other Aedes, I'd felt enough power that I could sustain fire for maybe a day, but with Kellan, it was different. I felt like I was charged up to go for a month straight.

I stumbled back a step and grabbed on to Kellan's other

arm for support. For a second, I was so overwhelmed that I forgot Kellan was my partner. Then I looked up into his eyes, and it hit me.

We're compatible.

He had the same look of shock in his eyes, like he'd felt it, too.

That doesn't seem right.

The sensation only lasted a second before my essence channel slammed shut again. Kellan seemed to sense it.

"Relax, Cora," he said as I found my balance again.

My cheeks flamed red, and I couldn't meet his gaze. I was still trying to process the sensation I'd just felt. It was the same as always… but different, too. Stronger. A helluva lot stronger. How was this possible for the two of us?

I kept my eyes on my rat and said, "I can't."

It was true. If that channel opened up the same way again, there's no way I could relax. It was just too much stimulation at once.

"Why not?" he asked, dropping his hand to his side. I couldn't read his tone.

"Because I don't think we can work together," I admitted.

Kellan looked totally taken aback, then started laughing lightly. All the other teams were chatting, so nobody but me heard him.

"You don't want to work with me?" he asked in amusement.

I finally looked him in the eyes. He was smirking at me, like this whole thing was a game to him. I couldn't work with someone who didn't take this class seriously.

"I know you don't like me," I snapped.

His laughter died. "What gave you that impression?"

I crossed my arms. "I heard what you said about me. You don't think I have what it takes to pass."

Kellan shrugged. "Why do you care what I say?"

I opened my mouth to say something, but then his question truly hit me. I stood there with my mouth agape, unanswering. Why *did* I care?

I shook it off. "Whatever. I don't."

"Really?" he asked. "Because you sound like you do."

I was starting to get irritated. "Look, you don't know me. So if you could just leave me alone and let me study in peace, that'd be great."

He held his hands up in surrender, but he looked like he was enjoying this more than anything. "Agreed. I'll leave you alone—after we finish this assignment. We still have a few minutes left to see if this works."

I scoffed. "With you? Oh, fun. Considering you have no faith in me at all."

Kellan leaned in and whispered, "So prove me wrong."

"Excuse me?" I asked.

He shrugged. "Prove me wrong. Show me you have what it takes to heal."

Oh, it was on! Kellan was wrong about me. I belonged here at the academy, and I was going to graduate top of my class. Kellan—or anyone else for that matter—couldn't stop me.

"Fine," I said confidently, but my heart was racing. "Let's go again."

Kellan placed his hand back on my shoulder. This time,

the essence current wasn't as overwhelming, but it was still strong. I could feel the channel opening wider and wider with each passing second. My fingers began to glow, but when I let out a cheerful gasp, they dimmed again.

Kellan leaned into me, until his chest was pressed against the side of my arm. The contact helped open the channel even more. "Relax, Cora," he reminded me softly.

I took a deep breath and forced the tension out of my shoulders. Essence traveled down my arms and to my hand. I held back on it since the rat was so small, and directed it only through the tips of my fingers. I tried to employ the techniques Professor Kovski had taught us in class, about how to visualize the healing process before it ever happened.

Right before my eyes, the incision began to glow. The skin began to knit itself together, and then...

Then the incision was gone. The skin was completely healed.

Kellan dropped his hand, and I felt my essence pull back. It was still there and a lot stronger than before, but not like it was when he was touching me.

I couldn't believe it. I stared down at the rat and ran my fingers over the stitches, but that was all that was left. The incision hadn't even scarred.

"Oh my God," I whispered.

When I finally lifted my gaze to Kellan, he looked impressed. He was speechless.

"I-I did it," I said breathlessly.

Kellan's surprise melted from his face, and it turned into a frown. "*We* did it," he clarified.

"Right," I agreed quickly. "We—"

"Very good job!" Professor Sanders said, clapping me on the back. "This looks excellent. Professor Kovski, if you would."

Kovski stepped up to our table and did the same thing she had with Celina's rat. A smile spread across her face, and pride filled my chest.

"Excellent work," she said as she pulled her hand back. "There are no internal injuries. It's rare for us to see such a great team on the first day. You two should be proud of yourselves. We only have a few minutes left, so you're free to leave for the day."

Kellan and I exchanged a glance as our professors moved on to the next table. Kellan looked a little shocked, then smiled at me.

"How's that for proving you wrong?" I asked with a proud smirk.

"I'm impressed," he admitted, "but I don't take back what I said."

My jaw dropped. "You heard what Professor Kovski said. I healed this rat without any complications."

Kellan winced, like I'd said something wrong. "There's a lot more to healing than this."

I crossed my arms and glared at him. "Yeah, and that's what I'm here at the academy to learn. Clearly, I'm capable of something, or that rat wouldn't be healed right now."

Kellan reached down and grabbed his bag, which he slung over his shoulder. "I'm sure you'll do fine, Cora. Forget I said anything."

Kellan started for the door, and I quickly grabbed my bag and followed behind him. I'd meet up with Laura later.

"Forget it?" I asked when we were out in the hall.

He didn't even turn to look back at me. I quickened my step to walk beside him.

"But what if we're paired up?" I demanded.

"You heard Kovski," he said coolly. "Just because we did well today doesn't mean we're going to be paired up."

"It kind of increases our chances, though," I pointed out.

Kellan glanced down at me, then turned his gaze forward again. "Trust me, they're not going to pair us up if we don't want to be."

"Well, good," I snapped. "Because you're kind of a jackass."

"And you're a little irritating," he deadpanned. "We all have our flaws. See you later."

Kellan and I reached the front doors of the Elemental Building, and he pushed through them to outside. I'd had enough of him. I stopped inside the doors, fuming as I watched him go.

"Screw you, Kellan Green," I called before the door swung shut.

He gave a salute, like he didn't even care.

"Whatever," I mumbled under my breath. "I hope you and your partner are freaking happy."

As long as that partner wasn't me, everything would be a-okay.

6

"I got my assignment!" Laura said excitedly.

I was sitting in a study area in the Academy Center three weeks later when she rushed up to me. My laptop was set on the table in front of me, and I was studying for my Elemental Magic exam the following week. I tossed a flaming ball of fire from one palm to the other, following the instructions in our study guide.

I killed the flames when Laura sat across from me. "You did? Congratulations!"

"His name is Travis Marcos," she said.

"I don't think I've met him," I told her.

"I don't think so, either," she replied. "He's in the other time block for lecture, but we met during that testing I had scheduled last Thursday. We hit it off, and I guess we're almost a perfect match. He even has earth element like me, so I've decided to major in natural disasters with him."

I frowned. "I'm never going to get an assignment."

Laura sighed. "Don't say that, Cora. Kovski said it can take weeks."

"But almost everyone is already paired up," I pointed out. "I barely showed promise with anyone, and the ones I did are already assigned. Shaylene and I would've been great together. She's even in the firefighting program. But she's with a guy from the other lecture block."

"What about Kellan?" Laura asked.

"Kellan's impossible," I said. "He has some serious issues. I'm not going to be paired with him."

"You should give him a shot," she encouraged. "He doesn't seem all bad."

"Just *some* bad?" I joked. I quickly changed the subject. "So, this Travis guy, is he Aedes or Davina?"

"Davina," Laura said. "I'll be doing the Aedes part with him."

"Good. It's just too bad we didn't get paired up," I complained. "We weren't half bad together after that first day."

"Yeah, but they look at more than just that," Laura pointed out. "Those personality tests weren't for nothing. And they look at your major—"

She was cut off by the sound of a notification on my computer. We both froze and exchanged a glance, like we could sense exactly what email had just come through.

I quickly looked to see that Professor Kovski had just emailed me. *Congratulations! You've Been Assigned*, the subject line read. My heart started to beat so fast that my fingers trembled.

"Is it—?" Laura started.

"Yes, oh my God. It is." I quickly opened the email and scanned it, until I found the name of my partner in the middle of the email. My stomach bottomed out.

"Holy shit," I muttered.

"What?" Laura asked eagerly. "Who'd you get?"

I didn't answer right away. I was still trying to convince myself it wasn't real.

"Come on, Cora," Laura pressed. "Who is it? Someone you know?"

"Yeah." My mouth felt dry and scratchy when I answered. "It's Kellan."

"Congratulations!" she cried.

"No," I said dryly. I crossed my arms and leaned back in my chair. "Not congratulations. This is a disaster. Kellan hates me. I can't work with him."

"Is it really that bad?" she asked.

I shrugged. "I don't know. Ask him what his problem is."

"So, contest it," Laura suggested, like people did that all the time.

"Contest it? Can I do that?"

"I don't know," she admitted. "Might as well try."

"You're right." I shut my laptop and shoved it in my bag, then stood. "I'm going to talk to Kovski now. I'll see you later."

"Good luck," Laura called as I started down the hall.

Professor Kovski's office was on the second floor of the Academy Center. I skipped the elevator and marched straight up the stairs to her office.

When I arrived, her door was open, and I could hear voices flooding out into the hall.

"It's very rare to refuse your assignment," Professor Kovski was saying, "but it can be done. We'll just need reasonable cause to know why you two can't work together."

Oh, good, I thought. *Kellan and I won't be the only ones contesting our assignment. Kovski will have to accommodate us.*

"She's unbearable," I heard a male voice say, and my jaw dropped. *Kellan?*

"I'm sorry, Mister Greene, but that's not—" Professor Kovski started to say, but she cut off when she saw me in the doorway.

Kellan glanced to me, and he looked like a deer in the headlights.

That's right. I've caught you talking shit a second time. What do you have to say for yourself?

I didn't say any of that. Instead, I said, "Kellan's right. We can't work together."

"Come in, Miss Marek," Professor Kovski said as she stood. She headed for the door and closed it behind me. "Why don't you both have a seat and tell me what's going on?"

I sat, but I crossed my arms to make it clear how much I objected to this assignment. "I don't know, Kellan. Why don't you tell her how much you hate me?"

Kellan sat, but he didn't look happy about it. "I don't *hate* you. I just… don't want to work with you."

"Why not?" I demanded, straightening in my seat. "What is it that you have against me? Is it something I said during that icebreaker? Because frankly, you've been an ass ever since, and I don't know why."

"Because it's obvious you're only here for one thing, and that's yourself," he snapped.

"How's that a bad thing?" I growled. "At least I *want* to be here. I *want* to help people. You act like you'd rather be doing anything else—"

"Well, maybe I do," he snarled back.

"Okay, okay," Professor Kovski said calmly. "One at a time. Cora, how about you go first?"

I felt like I could explode, but I kept my cool. "I think this must be some sort of mistake. Kellan has made it very clear that he has a stick up his ass, and I can't—"

"Whoa," Kellan cut in. "I do *not* have a stick up my—"

"Please, both of you calm down," Kovski demanded. She looked to me to continue.

I huffed. The truth was, I didn't know what it was about Kellan. He was just an ass.

"He's arrogant," I said, but that was all I could come up with.

"And Kellan?" Kovski asked. "What's your problem with Miss Marek?"

He answered without even having to think about it. "She's stuck up."

"I am not!" I defended. "Do you not like me because I'm a legacy? Well, news, *son of Ronan Greene*, so are you."

"That's not it," he shot back. "You don't work well with others, and that's been apparent since day one."

"That's not true," I insisted. "It's just *you* I can't work with."

Professor Kovski pressed her fingers to her temples. "Can't you two at least *try* to get along?"

"Why can't we just be reassigned?" I asked.

She dropped her hands and folded them on her desk. "Because you two showed the most promise than any other pairing we could come up with."

"I performed well with Celina," Kellan pointed out.

"Yes, but she performed better with Rhys, and they've already been paired up," Kovski said. "You two didn't just perform very well in class. You're also a match on the personality tests, and you're majoring in the same field. On paper, you're the perfect match."

"I'm still undecided," Kellan said.

Kovski frowned. "That's not what your file says."

"Yeah, well, I'm changing my mind," Kellan claimed.

My jaw dropped. This was bullshit.

Professor Kovski sighed and stood. "Look, you haven't given me a real reason to reconsider this pairing, so I'm afraid we're going to have to escalate this matter. Follow me."

She opened the door and breezed out of the room. Kellan and I exchanged a quick confused glance before both rushing to follow behind her.

"Where are we going?" I asked.

Her heels clicked against the tile. "It doesn't appear that I can help. I'm taking you to someone who can."

We ascended the stairs and came to a pair of double doors at the end of the hallway. A reception desk sat in front of them. Kovski stopped and told us to stay where we were, then stepped forward to talk to the secretary.

"Is Chancellor Harris available?" she asked in a low voice, so low that I could hardly make out their conversation.

My gaze shot up to Kellan's. "Did she just say Chancellor Harris?"

He kept his arms crossed and didn't look down at me. "Sounded like it to me."

The secretary pulled the phone to her ear. She said a few things into it that I couldn't hear, then stood and said, "Follow me."

She guided us through the double doors. We entered a large office with tall bookcases, wooden accents, and a huge mahogany desk in front of a wide window that over-looked the courtyard.

Chancellor Harris stood from her desk, and Kellan and I both froze in the doorway. "Come in," she said kindly, gesturing us to step forward after Professor Kovski. "Please, have a seat."

I nervously took the chair across from her, and Kellan sat in the one beside me. Professor Kovski remained on her feet.

"Chancellor Harris," Professor Kovski greeted as the secretary closed the doors behind us. "These are my students, Kellan Greene and Cora Marek."

Chancellor Harris stretched her hand out over the desk to shake my hand, then Kellan's. "It's so great to meet you. I knew both of your parents very well."

"It's great to meet you, too," I said kindly.

"What seems to be the problem?" Chancellor Harris asked.

Professor Kovski explained how we both refused to go through with the pairing. "Unfortunately," she concluded with, "most other students have been paired up, and I just don't see the alternative."

Chancellor Harris frowned. "You both realize what will happen if you don't accept this pairing?"

"What will happen?" I asked curiously.

She sighed. "You will have to go through with the semester alone."

"Great. Let's do it," I said quickly.

Chancellor Harris continued. "Our classes are not designed for individuals. They are designed for teams. You might pass your written exams, but without a partner, you have no hope of passing the practicals or your final."

"Fail the final?" I balked.

"You're both in the firefighting program," Chancellor Harris pointed out. "As I'm sure you're well aware, your final will consist of grueling obstacles inside a burning building. I'm afraid it would be too dangerous without a partner."

"So that's my only choice?" I asked. "I work with Kellan, or I flunk out of the academy?"

Chancellor Harris seemed sympathetic. "It's possible that we can find another partner for the two of you, but we'll have to see how the other teams perform first. If another team is not working well, we can reconsider swapping the pairings. But I'm confident in Professor Kovski's assignments. She is very good at what she does. I suggest the two of you spend some time together, get to know each other. If it doesn't work out by the end of the semester, we'll reconsider things."

"The end of the semester?" Kellan sounded just as hopeless as I felt. "What if we can't get along enough to pass by then?"

Chancellor Harris looked disappointed in us. "If your preliminary tests showed that the two of you can heal, I'm not sure what you have to worry about. I suggest you find some way to get along."

Kellan dropped his shoulders. He looked to me, like he was finally giving in. It wasn't like we had any other choice. Chancellor Harris was the ultimate voice at the academy. If she said we were locked into this assignment, we were locked in—unless one of us wanted to drop out.

No way in hell.

"We'll try," Kellan said, like he actually meant it.

He turned to me, expecting my answer. I had to agree with him—because there wasn't any other choice. Kellan and I were hopeless. It was go through with this, or fail, and I wasn't going to do that.

So I was just going to have to suffer through this semester, pass, and then wait for a reassignment when our final was over with. My dream of graduating top of the class had effectively been crushed, but without a partner, I wouldn't graduate at all.

"I guess we have no other choice," I said to Kellan, then I turned back to Chancellor Harris. "We'll try our best."

And I meant it. The only problem was, I wasn't sure that Kellan did.

7

"I don't get this guy," I complained to Laura later that evening. I lay on my bed in our dorm, picking at a thread on my blanket.

"I'm sure it'll be fine," she said, turning to check out her shoes in the mirror. She wore a short, sleek black dress and four-inch heels. "They wouldn't have paired you up if they didn't think you'd work well together."

I frowned. "They paired us up because we were the last two without partners."

Laura turned from the mirror to look at me. "Chancellor Harris said you could switch partners next semester, right?"

I pushed myself to a sitting position. "Yes. I'm going to do my best to work with him. I think I'm just… nervous. I don't really know the guy."

Laura came to sit beside me on the bed. "There's your solution. You have to get to know him."

I reached for my phone. "Okay, let's stalk his social media."

Laura chuckled. "Not like that. Talk to him. Figure out why he's such an ass."

I laughed. "I think I can do that."

"Perfect," she said with a smile. "Now, are you going to get dressed and come to the party with me?"

"You sure you wouldn't rather study?" I asked, only half-serious.

Laura nudged me. "It's Friday. You need to get out and forget about Kellan for the night."

I fake groaned and got to my feet. "Okay, you've twisted my arm. I'll go."

I stripped off my boots and placed the Davina Blade I kept there on my desk beside my antiques collection. There were things like buttons, pocket watches, jewelry, and an old silver bowl that belonged to my great-great grandmother. Laura's eyes widened when she saw the blade.

"Is that a Davina Blade?" she asked breathlessly.

I nodded shyly.

"As in, one of the ancient blades that came from Vehena?" she asked. "That the Davina once used as weapons against the Aedes?"

"Yeah," I admitted. "My uncle Kyle gave it to me. It kind of started my antiques collection."

She reached her hand out. "May I?"

I handed her the blade, and she looked it over in wonder.

"You're not really supposed to have weapons on campus," she said with a chuckle, "but this is really cool."

I shrugged. "Who's going to notice? I'm not going to hurt anyone with it. It's just sentimental to me."

She set the blade back on my desk. "Your collection is really cool."

"Thanks," I said. "I'll collect anything with a story behind it."

"Well, let's go make our own story," she said, beaming.

I dressed in a summery navy-blue dress with tiny pink flowers all over it. Laura let me borrow a pair of fancy sandals to go along with it. I wore my brown hair down in waves and added a light layer of makeup.

We took the city bus several blocks away until we came to a residential area. We followed the sound of music as a pumping bass pounded through the street. Hoards of people stood in front of a big white house with a towering turret on one corner. Lights flashed inside, and I could hear the sound of cheers above the music. Next to the house, the garage door was open, and a group of guys were playing beer pong on a fold-out table.

"I'm the king of the world!" a guy shouted as he burst out of the front door in nothing but his underwear and a red cape. He jumped over the porch banister and raced down the street. A group of guys hurried outside behind him, cheering and hollering as he streaked down the side-walk. Most of them held up their phones to film.

Laura and I stopped in our tracks. I turned to her in uncontrollable laughter. "Oh my God."

"*Somebody's* a little drunk," Laura said with raised eyebrows.

I grabbed her hand. "Come on."

Laura and I stepped inside, where the music was deafening. The living room was crowded, though people more or less milled around chatting instead of dancing to the music. When we got to the kitchen to find drinks, a Davina guy was standing on the counter shirtless and with his wings out.

Another guy reached up and tugged on his arm. "Put your wings away, Jett!" he demanded. "Do you *want* the neighbors to see? The Alliance will be all over your ass, and my parents will kill me."

"Save it for campus!" a girl shouted up at him.

Jett sighed and relaxed his shoulders, and his wings disappeared. "Screw you," he said lightheartedly. "You're no fun."

Laura and I maneuvered past a group chatting—I thought I heard the word *infantry*—and grabbed some wine coolers from the fridge, before she led me down a hall that opened to the garage. It was quieter out here, and I preferred that.

We arrived just as two guys were finishing up their game of beer pong. One had a single cup left, and the other guy sank the ball in. He shot his hands into the air in victory, while the other guy groaned and chugged his beer.

"Travis!" Laura hurried over to the guy who'd won. He was tall, with dark hair and kind eyes.

"Laura, you made it!" he said in excitement, though he seemed like he'd already had a few.

"Travis, this is my roommate, Cora," Laura introduced. "Cora, this is my partner, Travis."

"Hey," he greeted with a smile. "It's nice to meet you."

"You, too," I said.

"Looks like you're having fun," Laura told Travis. It almost sounded like she was flirting.

Girl, don't get involved with your partner. What if you break up?

"Reigning champion of the night," Travis said cheerfully. "Have you come to challenge me?"

Laura laughed. "Uh, no. I can't play to save my life. We're just here to watch."

He shrugged. "Suit yourself. Who's up next?"

"I'll go." Kellan's voice came from out on the lawn. I hadn't even noticed him until now, and I didn't think he'd seen me. I took a step back into the shadows.

"But Kellan," Celina complained from beside him. "I thought we were going to get drinks."

"I'll take you," the guy beside her said. He was all muscle and a head taller than Kellan. He was kind of scary-looking.

"Aw, thanks Rhys." Celina's eyes sparkling up at him.

I leaned over to Laura and whispered, "That's her partner?"

She nodded. "They seem like total opposites, right?"

I just shrugged. I didn't know enough about Celina to say one way or the other.

Travis clapped his hands and rubbed them together. "Okay, Kellan Greene. Prepare to have your ass handed to you."

Kellan smirked as he arranged his cups on the table. "Don't get too cocky, Travis. You haven't seen me play yet."

"Oh no," Travis feigned dryly. "I'm so scared."

"You should be," Kellan challenged with a smile.

Kellan blew on his ping pong ball for good luck, then tossed it across the table. It landed square in one of Travis's cups before he even finished arranging them. Travis's eyes widened, then his lips formed into a playful smirk.

"That's it." Travis held his hand out to the guy beside him but didn't take his eyes off Kellan. "Caleb, it's time for the lucky underwear."

"Are you sure?" Caleb asked. He was shorter than Travis, with dark skin, tight black curls, and an attractive smile. I was pretty sure he was the guy Shaylene had been partnered with. "It's still early in the night."

"Do it! Do it! Do it!" The garage broke out into a chorus of chants.

"I want to see this," I whispered to Laura, before joining in on the cheers. "Do it! Do it!"

"Should I?" Caleb asked for show. "Should I do it?"

He held up a backpack and slowly reached inside. "Here it comes. Are you ready?"

"Do it! Do it!" The chanting continued.

Caleb whipped a pair of golden spandex underwear out of the bag and held them up like a victory flag. The crowd broke out into cheers and applause.

"The lucky underwear!" Caleb shouted, waving them around.

He handed them to Travis, who pulled them on over his jeans. Several people cat-called, and Travis turned around to show them off. He held his hands in the air and gestured for more applause. Laura stuck her fingers in her mouth and whistled loudly.

"Oh my God!" I grabbed on to Laura's shoulder as I doubled over in laughter. "He's hilarious."

"I know." She beamed. "Isn't he great?"

Laura's eyes sparkled when she looked at him, and I could already tell she was crushing on him. Travis caught her eye and winked at her. Their connection was undeniable.

The crowd quieted as Travis stepped up to the table. "Think you can one-up this, Greene?"

Kellan shrugged. "I've got all the guns I need, Captain Underpants."

Kellan flexed his biceps, and the garage broke out into cheers again. I even found myself cheering for him.

"I don't know why you don't like Kellan," Laura said to me. "He seems fine."

I shrugged, unable to take my eyes off him. He seemed so confident, which I found both attractive and repulsive at the same time.

Kellan's eyes met mine, but he looked away quickly, like he hadn't noticed me. I finally turned my gaze away as the game started, so he wouldn't think I was staring. But when I looked out the door and over the lawn, I saw something that made my gut sink. I threw myself behind Laura.

"What?" she asked curiously. She stepped aside, and I quickly followed to stay hidden.

"Um... I just saw someone I know," I admitted.

"Well, why are you hiding? Go say hello."

I bit my lower lip. "I-I can't."

She tilted her head in question. My eyes stayed fixed to the guy with curly black hair as he strutted up the lawn. His arm was around a girl that kind of looked like me, and I felt a pang of envy stab my gut.

Laura followed my gaze, but he was out of sight the next second. "Who is he, Cora?"

I relaxed and stepped out from behind her. "It's Drew, my boyfriend from high school."

I'd told her about him weeks ago. I knew Drew was attending the academy, but I'd done all I could to avoid him so far. Things hadn't ended well between us. The only solace I found was knowing we wouldn't be paired up since we were both Davina.

Laura's eyes widened. "*He's* the guy who—?"

"Used me for sex then stomped on my heart?" I finished for her. "Yep."

Her shoulders fell. "Cora, I'm so sorry."

I shook it off. "No, it's fine. It happened over a year ago."

"That doesn't make what he did okay," she said. "If you want, I can go spill my drink on him."

I laughed. "No, it's cool. Besides, you'd ruin your shoes."

She glanced to her feet. "Good point."

Laura and I stayed to watch the rest of the beer pong match. It was really close, with each of them getting down to only one cup, but eventually, Travis won. He shot his hands into the air, then did a victory dance, before pulling on the golden spandex waistband and letting it snap back against his jeans.

Kellan chuckled. "I guess those really do hold some power."

Travis took a swig of beer. "These panties are undefeated, sweetheart."

"Good game, bro," Kellan said, shaking Travis's hand.

Travis patted Kellan on the back, though he swayed a little on his feet. "Okay, losers. Who's up next?"

Laura quickly rushed over to him. "Travis, I think you've had enough. Let's take a break."

He waved his hand. "Nah, I can keep going."

"Travis," she persisted.

Travis burped, then clutched his stomach. The color drained from his face. "Okay, partner. You might be right."

He turned and hightailed it inside, making a mad dash to the bathroom.

The garage went silent for a second before Caleb said, "Okay, who's up next?"

I followed Laura and Travis inside. Laura sat on the edge of the tub, rubbing Travis's back while he puked into the toilet.

"Is he going to be okay?" I asked from the doorway.

"Totally fine," she assured me.

Travis gave a thumbs-up, then started retching again.

I couldn't watch, so I turned from the door and started for the kitchen to wait for Laura. I tossed my empty bottle into the recycling, then grabbed another drink from the fridge. I noticed the music had changed, and it sounded like someone was singing karaoke—and really well, too. I decided to check it out and stopped in the doorway to the living room.

It was Celina. She was standing on the coffee table with a microphone in her hand while words played across the TV. People were cheering for her. She swayed her hips while she sang and held one hand into the air, creating a swirling display of fire above her head. She was in the fire-fighting program like me, but I only had her in a few classes.

"She's good, isn't she?" a male voice asked.

I turned to see that Kellan had come up beside me. "I-I guess so," I stammered. What was I saying? She was amazing. "Do you know her well?"

"We went to high school together," Kellan told me over the loud music.

I quickly realized this was my opportunity to get to know him better, but I didn't know what to say. The guy was intimidating as hell.

"So, you two are dating?" I asked. I wanted to shove the words back in my mouth.

Kellan took a swig of beer, then chuckled. "Uh, no."

I couldn't read his tone. It was almost like if it were up to him, they would be dating. He certainly couldn't take his eyes off of her.

"So, um, where'd you go to high school?" I asked, but it came off nervous-sounding.

"Jackson High," Kellan said, then quickly added, "in Iowa."

"Oh, right," I said. "I've heard of it. I went to Galen High in Eagle Valley."

Kellan nodded, like he already knew. "Sounds cool. I've always wanted to visit the site of the Malum portal. Haven't had the chance yet."

I shrugged. "It's just a bunch of rocks. Nothing special."

He didn't respond. Silence settled between us, but I couldn't take it.

"Hey, since we're partners and all, maybe we should think about scheduling some study sessions," I suggested. "You know, to get to know each other."

"Sure," he agreed, but he was still looking up at Celina while she performed. "Just name the time and place."

"We could meet Monday after class, like three o'clock in the Activities Center," I said.

He shrugged again. "Sure, sounds good."

Celina finished, and the living room broke out into cheers. She handed off the microphone to Shaylene, who was wearing skin-tight jeans and looked ready to put on a show. Rhys reached up to help Celina down from the coffee table, then handed her a drink. She fell into his arms, laughing.

"How was it, Rhys?" she asked him. "Was it good?"

"It was great," he said. "You're really talented."

She smacked him playfully. "Oh, stop."

Kellan's eyes darkened from beside me. He was obviously jealous. "Hey, Celina!"

She looked over to us and waved. She quickly pushed through the crowd and stopped in front of us. "Kellan! Where have you been?"

"Playing beer pong," he said, like it was obvious.

"It took you that long?" she said with a fake pout.

Kellan shot a glance at Rhys, then took Celina's hand. "Maybe we can go get that drink now."

"No worries!" she said chipperly, holding up a plastic cup. "Rhys already got me one. Who's this?"

She looked over to me, eyeing me up and down. I suddenly felt like I should be pulling her hair out or something. I didn't like the way she looked at me.

"Nobody," Kellan said casually, and my stomach sank. "Just my partner."

Celina's face lit up. "Oh, *you're* Cora Marek. Of course. I should've known. I'm Celina Dyer. Perhaps you've heard of me?"

She stuck her hand out, and I had no choice but to shake it.

"Yeah, Kellan's mentioned you," I said. She was so fake I could hardly stand it.

Celina giggled, then swatted Kellan in the shoulder. "Kellan, you talk about me?"

"Only good things," he teased.

Ugh. Gag. This flirting was more uncomfortable than Travis's barfing.

"I'll see you on Monday," I said to Kellan before turning toward the hall to get away from them.

"Wait, Cora!" Celina called, following me.

I stopped in the doorway to the kitchen. Though we weren't far from Kellan and Rhys, they couldn't hear us over Shaylene's singing.

"Yeah?" I asked as politely as I could manage.

"Look…" I could hear the fake kindness in her voice. "Kellan and I kind of have a thing going."

I laughed out loud. "Oh, God. You don't have to worry about us. We're changing partners by the end of the semester."

"See, that's the thing," she said carefully, like she was speaking to a child. "I want Kellan to stay in school with me, so let's make one thing clear. You *better* work your ass off for him. He *needs* to pass that final."

Oh, this bitch was *not* threatening me.

I took a step closer to her, finally feeling the alcohol kicking in and lowering my inhibitions. Yeah, I was a light-weight—so sue me. "And what are you going to do about it if he fails?"

Celina's gaze roamed over me, but that threat never left her eyes. "I'll make sure you never return to the academy."

I scoffed. Was she serious?

"Relax," I said, rolling my eyes. "I want to pass as much as he does. By the end of the semester, Kellan and I are going to be the best team Harris Academy has ever seen."

Celina smirked. "Oh, that I would very much like to see, considering Rhys and I are already working on that title. But have fun trying."

I didn't back down. I raised my eyebrows and stepped toward her, until we were almost touching. "Bitch, it is on."

Celina's lips twitched. "I always did like a little competition."

Before I could say anything more, she whirled around and started back toward Kellan and Rhys. Kellan's eyes darted between the two of us, like he couldn't figure out what that was all about. I shot him a half-hearted smile, but inside, I was reeling.

Celina thought she could threaten me? Well, fine. I was up to the challenge. My team was going to blow all others out of the water.

I just needed to get Kellan on board.

8

I paced nervously in the entrance to the Activities Center the following Monday after class. Kellan was fifteen minutes late, and I was starting to get a little peeved. We'd talked earlier that day in our Introduction to Firefighting class, so I knew he wasn't out sick. I glanced down at my phone. I would've messaged him, but he still hadn't accepted my friend request online, and I didn't have his phone number.

I was starting to hope he was waiting for me at a different entrance and hadn't completely blown me off, but as the minutes ticked by, the more I realized that was unlikely. This was the obvious place to meet. A half an hour passed, and then forty-five minutes. I huffed and finally gave up.

I stomped out of the Activities Center and across the lawn toward the dining hall, where I knew I'd find Laura. The cafeteria was huge, with a maze of tables and a long buffet line. Huge floor-to-ceiling windows lined the outer wall, letting in the sunshine. It was the end of September, so it was one of the last nice days we might have.

I piled my plate with food from the salad bar, then found Laura sitting at a table in the corner beside Travis, Caleb, and Shaylene. They were discussing anatomy homework and arguing over which bone was the radius and which was the ulna.

"Your radius is this bone," Laura insisted. She ran her fingers over her forearm, drawing an invisible line down to her thumb.

"Are you sure?" Caleb asked, giving her a quizzical look.

"Positive," Laura replied.

He glanced to Shaylene beside him for confirmation.

"She's right," Shaylene said. "Didn't we go over this last night?"

Caleb held back a smile. "I was, uh, a little distracted."

Shaylene blushed and wiggled her eyebrows. "*Yeah* you were."

It was no secret that those two had hit it off the moment they'd been paired up.

Travis took immediate interest. "Ooh, give us the details."

"Get lost." Shaylene shoved Travis playfully.

Laura's gaze darted up to mine as I sat across from her. "Oh, hey Cora."

I smiled. "Hi."

Shaylene had made it clear to Travis he wasn't getting any details of last night. He gave up and turned to Laura. "Okay, smarty pants. You seem pretty confident you're going to ace this test. What's this called?"

Travis pointed to his elbow. Without hesitation, Laura answered, "Olecranon process."

Travis frowned. "I was hoping you'd forget that one."

She shrugged. "I study."

"So, can you take this test for us?" Caleb joked.

"Sure," Laura said casually. "If you want to be kicked out of the academy for cheating."

Caleb's face fell. "Flash cards, it is."

Laura giggled, then turned to me. "What's up? I thought you were meeting with Kellan tonight."

I pursued my lips. "I was *supposed* to, but he never showed."

"What a jerk," Laura said lightheartedly.

"He is," I laughed. "At least I'm trying to make an effort. I can't do all the work for him."

"I hope nothing happened to him," she said in concern. "I hope he's okay."

"It's Kellan Greene," I pointed out. "I'm sure he's fine."

Travis's voice cut through our conversation. "Hey, Laura. What's the kneecap called again?"

"Patella," she answered. "We've gone over this at least fifteen times."

"Right," Travis replied. "We might need an extra study session before Thursday's test. My dorm room?"

Laura shrugged. "Sure."

Travis turned back to Caleb and Shaylene, and I gave Laura a wide-eyed look.

"What?" she asked innocently.

I whispered quietly, though Travis was ignoring us. "He

did *not* forget what the kneecap is called. He just wants to get you alone."

Laura turned bright pink, then her lips formed into a smile. "I don't have a problem with that at all."

I nudged her with my foot playfully under the table. "Don't have too much fun."

Laura smirked at me. "Please. We're partners. We're not dating."

"Yet," I added for her.

"Shh…" she hissed, glancing to Travis, but he was still talking to Caleb and didn't hear us. She straightened in her seat. "What will you be doing tonight?"

I poked at my food. "Probably studying. And hoping I don't fail the semester."

I gave a nervous chuckle, but the sad part was that it was true.

My stomach sank when Kellan entered our anatomy classroom the following morning. Laura, Shaylene, and I were seated beside each other toward the front. My eyes followed Kellan all the way to the back, until he slid into the empty seat beside Celina. He had a cocky smirk on his face and didn't even bother a glance my way.

I started to stand, but Laura tugged on my wing.

"Where are you going?" she asked.

"To confront Kellan," I said. "He stood me up."

Before I could start down the row of chairs, Professor Braff entered the room. I sighed and returned to my seat.

Short of pulling Kellan out of the room and chewing him out in the hall, I wouldn't get a word in with him before class started.

"Okay, everyone," Professor Braff said as he stopped at the front of the room. The class quieted. "Get out a pencil. Pop quiz."

The entire class let out a collective groan, and Professor Braff laughed. "Kidding, but it sounds like most of you aren't ready for the test later this week. And I'll tell you why that's a big mistake."

Professor Braff was younger than most of our professors and had a great sense of humor. He was my favorite professor.

He continued. "As you may have noticed by now, attendance makes up ten percent of your grade. And still, many of you see it fit to skip my class."

He shoved his hands into his pockets and stared out at our faces with a pointed expression. He'd dropped his sense of humor and was getting serious now. It was strange, to say the least.

"We've spent the last two weeks studying the bones of the body. But why does it matter?" He paused for dramatic effect, though it was clear the question was rhetorical. "Every semester, I have at least one student come up to me and say, 'Professor, all these bones and muscles are too hard to remember. What do I have to know them for anyway?' And you know what I say? I say, 'You're right. I can't remember them either.'"

The class broke out into laughter.

Professor Braff's smile returned. "No, but seriously, you need to all understand why this class is important."

He continued to speak while he pulled up his slideshow presentation on the computer. "We all know that widespread chronic conditions are the most difficult to heal. Why do you think that is?"

Laura raised her hand.

"Yes, Miss Blake?" Professor Braff called on her.

"Healing requires the healer to target the area of treatment," Laura answered. "Without guidance and care, the essence that enters the body is useless, sometimes even damaging. The Davina administering the essence must be able to feel and target what they're healing."

"Precisely," Professor Braff said. "It's why lacerations are easy for us, because we can see the area that needs healing and focus on it. Once we get into internal injuries, such as broken bones or torn ligaments, things get trickier. You have to be able to identify which bone is broken, or which ligament needs healing. You target the wrong metatarsal, and you could injure your patient further."

Professor Braff changed the slide, and the entire room broke out into murmurs of disgust. The photograph he showed us displayed disfigured toes that were purple with bruises and twisted in unnatural directions. I remained calm. I was sure I'd see much worse than this in the field.

"As you can see, healing magic is as dangerous as it is helpful," Professor Braff pointed out. "So if you want to become a healer, don't blow off my class."

The whole room went silent for several seconds. I could

feel the tension in the air as he narrowed his eyes into the crowd.

Finally, Professor Braff turned on his heel and started for the whiteboard. "Moving on."

I swore I heard the class take a collective breath. I leaned over to Laura and whispered, "That was a little intense. Usually he's so laid back."

"Agreed," she whispered back. "But he's right. If we don't get this down, we'll never learn to heal."

She stared down at her open textbook with a terrified look on her face. I suddenly felt bad for her.

Shaylene seemed to notice and quickly said, "It's fine. We can all study together."

Laura would pass this class for sure, but what Professor Braff had said clearly made her nervous.

My hand shot into the air before I really thought about it. "Professor?"

He turned to me with a raised eyebrow. "Miss Marek?"

I dropped my hand to my desk. "Yeah, I was just wondering… If it's the Davina's task to find the site of the injury and do the actual healing, why is this topic important for Aedes?"

Professor Braff looked confused by my question, and I felt like I'd just asked the stupidest thing in the world. But it was a valid question, wasn't it?

"Because, Miss Marek," he said kindly, "the Aedes are there to help. You are partners, and though they don't do the actual healing part of things, they should be supporting their Davina partner in every way possible. At times, that may include confirming their diagnosis. Don't underestimate the power of your partner just because they have a different job than you."

With that, he began his lecture, and I was left considering his words. I'd been trying to ease some of Laura's nerves, but I didn't think it helped.

For the next hour, all I could hear was the sound of Professor Braff's voice echoing in my head. *Don't underestimate the power of your partner...*

It felt like a personal attack, like he knew Kellan and I weren't working well together. But was I *underestimating* him? I didn't know.

By the time class ended, I was ready to figure it out.

"Kellan!" I called down the hallway as the class dispersed. I told Laura to go on without me, then quickened my pace toward Kellan. He didn't hear me, so I called his name again.

He let out an exasperated sigh and stopped in the middle of the hallway. "What is it?"

He sounded like he was trying to be nice, but I could hear the irritation in his tone.

Celina looked me up and down, then said, "See you later, Kellan."

He shot her a quick wave and said, "Bye."

"What happened yesterday?" I asked him.

His eyebrows knitted together. "Yesterday?"

"Yeah, were you sick or something?" I was trying to be nice, but the way he looked at me—like just the sight of me made him want to vomit—suggested he blew me off on purpose. "We were supposed to meet up in the Activities Center to train."

"Shit, I totally forgot about that." His tone was totally unreadable.

I crossed my arms. I couldn't tell if he was being honest or not. "Really? Or are you trying to be difficult?"

"I'm not *trying* to be anything," he insisted, though it didn't sound like the accusation bothered him at all.

I raised an eyebrow. "You sure? Because you never wanted to be my partner in the first place. We're a terrible pair."

"On the contrary, we're the perfect pair," he argued.

I was speechless. All I could do was make a face at him.

"What do you mean?" I finally asked.

Kellan shrugged. "No big deal."

"It *is* a big deal," I snapped. By now, we were the only two left in the hall, so I didn't mind raising my voice. "This is our future we're talking about. Do you want to flunk out? Because I'm willing to put in the work so that doesn't happen, but I can't do it without your help. What's your deal, anyway?"

Kellan frowned. "I don't have a *deal*."

"Sure you do. Everyone does," I pointed out.

Kellan shifted his weight between his feet and looked away from me.

"Well…?" I pressed.

Kellan sighed, finally looking me in the eye. "Look, I'm sorry I ditched you. I really did forget."

He sounded like he was telling the truth.

"Fine," I said, accepting his excuse. "But from now on, we need to communicate better with each other. We're partners, and I know that doesn't mean much to you, but it means something to me."

"It *does* mean something to me," he argued, then held his hand out. "Give me your phone. I'll put my number in."

I unlocked my screen and handed him my phone. He entered his number, then handed it back.

"I really am sorry," he said softly. "Let me make it up to you. Can we meet later tonight?"

I pressed my lips together, trying to get a reading on him, but he was impossible. I couldn't tell if his offer was genuine or not. Finally, I said, "Yeah, I'm available after class."

"Okay," he said. "Let's meet up then."

He started walking away, but I quickly stopped him. "Hold on. Where should I meet you?"

He paused, then said, "My dorm? Clark Hall, room 313. Four o'clock?"

"Okay," I said reluctantly. I'll bring the ham."

He shot me a quizzical look. "Ham? For dinner?"

I rolled my eyes. "Lord, you've missed too many lectures. You'll see."

A smile passed his lips. "It should be interesting."

I wasn't amused, but I replied anyway. "Yeah, it should be."

9

*J*arrived at Kellan's dorm room at four o'clock on the dot. I knocked, and the door swung open.

"Come on in," Kellan said.

I followed him inside. It was quiet, since his roommate wasn't around.

Kellan's room was the same dimensions as mine, but apart from that, they looked nothing alike. All the furniture was set up in different spots, and he had a futon that faced a huge TV. For some reason, I expected his room to be a mess, but I was surprised to see that it was neat and tidy. On one side of the room, band posters were hung all over the wall, while the other side had a mural of a forest tacked from floor-to-ceiling.

Kellan sat on the side with the mural. I tried to take in everything I could about the room to see if I could figure out what his deal was, but it was all trivial. There was a pair of hiking boots at the foot of his bed, a basketball on the top of his dresser, and a fishing pole propped up in the corner.

"The suspense is killing me," Kellan said from the bed. "What's the ham for?"

I took a seat at his desk chair and pushed aside a thick law book and an empty takeout container of Pad Thai to make room. I placed the ham on the desk and began to peel back the plastic covering. "In one of Professor Kovski's lectures, she talked about using meat to practice on. It won't actually heal it, since it's not alive, but it gives something for us to channel our essence into. It'll help us practice while we get a feel for each other's power."

Kellan sat up a little straighter, looking intrigued. "So, what's the plan?"

"Suffer through this," I joked. I was relieved to hear him laugh a little in agreement. I quickly turned serious again. "I wanted to start with feeling our connection again, since we haven't had a chance to work together since that first lab. I was planning to do some elemental work in the Activities Center, but now that we're stuck here, it's probably best if we don't burn the dorm hall down."

Kellan smirked. "No, let's not do that."

"So instead, I thought we could try some healing techniques together," I said. "It's not going to do anything since we don't have a living being to practice on, but at least we can get the techniques down."

Kellan stood and came up beside me. "Okay. Let's see what we're capable of."

He placed a hand on my shoulder. My essence felt like a rocket whipping through my body and leaving behind a tingling trail of fire. For a second, it felt like Kellan had sucked all my essence energy out of me. Then it came flooding through me like the wall between the earth and my body had broken.

Essence flowed through me and into Kellan. He took a deep, calming breath, and I could tell it was energizing him.

Maybe he'll be more bearable once his essence energy is balanced, I thought.

"Our connection is really strong," I remarked. I was starting to see why Professor Kovski had partnered us up. Something about Kellan's power opened my channel wider than I'd ever felt it before. I could tell by the faraway look in his eyes that he felt it, too.

"Yeah," he said without looking at me. "I guess we do."

I was ready to get down to business. "Still, I need you to open my channel wider. I need to access more essence to heal."

I could feel the moment he began to siphon more, because the energy began to buzz throughout my body at a higher frequency. The feeling that came with it made me actually like Kellan a little more.

I waited until I felt the channel stop expanding, then closed my eyes and placed my hands over the ham. I guided my essence down my arms like I had during our class with the rats, then let it settle in the palms of my hands. I pushed just a little to test it out, but I could feel my hands heating from my fire.

"Do you want roasted ham for dinner?" I asked, only half-serious.

"It's free food, right?" Kellan chuckled.

"Yeah, but that's not the point," I said. "I need more essence for healing, or I'm going to fire-roast this ham. Can you pull any more?"

"I'll try," he said.

My essence intensified, and I felt the heat in my hands wane to nothing more than a warm, comforting sensation. I pushed more essence into my hands. When I opened my eyes, they were glowing.

"That's it!" I cried, but as soon as I said it, the glow shifted from white to a red burst of energy.

Kellan and I both jumped back. I nearly tipped the chair back, while he stumbled into the corner of the bed. My essence channel immediately waned, until all I could feel was a light buzz. It'd be enough to conjure fire for a few days, but definitely not enough to heal.

"I thought we weren't having fire-roasted ham for dinner," Kellan teased.

"Shut up," I shot back playfully. I looked down at my hands, wondering where I went wrong. "I know what I'm doing."

Kellan shifted uncomfortably between his feet. "If it's okay, can I give you some advice?"

I raised an eyebrow at him. "Says the guy who didn't know you could use a ham to practice your essence."

Kellan held his hands up in surrender. "Look, I know you have all the textbook stuff down. You know the technique. But putting it into practice is a lot different. There are things no professor can teach you; you have to figure them out on your own."

I sensed some sort of insult was coming on, but I had to remind myself that Kellan and I were in this together. I didn't have any intention of fighting with him.

Don't underestimate him, I reminded myself.

"So, what am I missing?" I asked, though my guts churned. I wasn't sure I was ready for the answer.

"Your emotions are getting in the way," Kellan said.

I crossed my arms. "Are you suggesting I don't know how to deal with my emotions?"

He shrugged. "I don't know. Do you? You're acting pretty defensive right now, and all I'm trying to do is help."

I quickly dropped my arms to my sides. "Okay, so what do I have to do?"

Kellan reached out for my shoulder again. "Try to forget that I'm here."

"Forget you exist," I said, making a check sign in the air. "Got it. I can do that."

"Ha ha," Kellan said dryly. "Don't let your feelings for me get in the way of your essence."

I took a deep breath. "Okay, let's try this again."

Kellan and I did as we'd done before. He drew my essence into himself, which opened up my channel wider and allowed me to gather more into my palms, but they barely glowed.

"I can feel you resisting against me." Kellan had his eyes closed and was focusing intently on the flow of essence between us. "You need to let your essence flow to me *and* to your palms. Don't divert it all to healing."

"But I need all I can get to heal," I pointed out.

"Let me take what I can, and you'll have plenty more to work with," he said.

I relaxed and tried to follow his instruction, but I couldn't feel my channel opening wider. It was like it was all flowing straight to him, and I needed more if I wanted to conjure healing essence.

"Cora," he pressed. "You're pulling away from me again. Don't resist."

I gave in, and I suddenly felt my channel opening wider. I gathered what I could and directed it down my arms and to my palms. My hands began to glow, but when I tried to transfer the energy into the ham, I couldn't make the transfer.

"Something's wrong," I said in frustration.

Kellan dropped his hand, and my essence pulled back as my channel shrank.

"What?" I asked in surprise.

"You're not following my instructions," he accused.

I looked up at him. "Yes, I was."

"It's not enough to give me just a piece of your essence," he explained. "You can't hold back. I'm not going to drain it from you, Cora. It doesn't work that way."

"Kellan, I did exactly what you asked," I said as I wiped my hands on my jeans. I was getting ham grease all over them and felt gross.

He shook his head. "But you didn't. I can feel it. I can sense the flow of essence through you. You're still holding back."

"If I am, I don't mean to." Irritation entered my tone again.

Kellan noticed. "Getting frustrated isn't going to help either of us."

"You're getting frustrated, too," I pointed out.

"Christ," Kellan sighed. "We've barely started, and we're already arguing."

"I don't think we're arguing," I said. "We just have to talk this out."

Kellan plopped onto his bed. "So, what's the problem? Why are you trying to do all this work alone? Why won't you let me do my part?"

"Maybe the problem isn't me," I suggested. I really tried to keep a level head, but it felt like he was accusing me of being incapable before we'd even gotten to the root of the problem. "Maybe you're not taking as much essence from me as you could be."

Kellan frowned. "That's ridiculous. Why would I do that?"

I shrugged. "I don't know. Because you've been doing the bare minimum all semester just to get by."

Kellan raked his fingers through his blond hair. He looked like he'd just about had enough of me today. "I'm trying the best I can. You're the one with healing power, so I think it's logical to work on that first."

"Yeah, I *am* the one with healing power, so why am I taking lessons from you?" I raised a challenging eyebrow.

Kellan's lips tightened. "Just because I don't have healing power doesn't mean I don't understand the theory behind it. I'm taking the same classes you are—"

"And you've missed half of them!" I exclaimed. He couldn't even argue with that, because it was true. "Don't even pretend like Professor Braff wasn't talking about you today when he chewed us out about attendance."

"My attendance has nothing to do with what I know," he defended. His eyebrows just kept falling deeper and deeper over his eyes.

It was clear we were both fed up with each other already. I stood and swung my bag over my shoulder. I left the ham behind on his desk. He could eat it for all I cared.

"Wait!" he demanded, shooting to his feet. "Where are you going?"

I whirled around before I got to the door. "Clearly, this isn't happening tonight. Let's take a break and try again later."

Kellan's shoulders fell. "Wait, Cora. I really want to try to work with you."

"So take some time to figure out what the deal is," I suggested. "You said it yourself. I have more power than you, which means I should be able to do this."

Kellan pressed his fingers to his eyes, like he was dealing with a migraine. He dropped his hands and rolled his eyes at me. "You really think that you're better than me because you're a Davina, don't you?"

I scowled at him. "I never said that."

"But you meant it," he accused, his voice rising.

"Your part is easy!" I shot back at him. "All you have to do is stand there while you fuel up on my essence. I'm the one who has to conjure healing essence, diagnose the issue, and heal without fucking it up. So sorry if I think my part is a little more involved than yours."

Kellan burst. "See? This is why we can't work together. Your head is too big!"

"And you're not dedicated enough!" I accused.

Kellan gritted his teeth and stared me down. I held his gaze.

"Fine," he snapped. "Just go. I thought you cared about passing this semester. I wanted to help you with that, but I can't if you're going to act this way."

"Act what way?" I snapped. *He* was the one being a major douchebag.

Kellan reached around me and swung the door open, then started pushing me out of the room. "Have fun trying to heal without me. Come back when you appreciate my role in this."

"Kellan," I protested as he shoved me out into the hallway. "Stop it. I never said I didn't appreciate you—"

He slammed the door in my face.

Fine. I wasn't going to stick around if he didn't want me here. I stormed down the hall, getting away from him as quickly as I could.

One training session down. Only three months of training with this asshole to go.

I couldn't stop replaying my encounter with Kellan the following day. I barely paid attention in my Art of Healing lecture, and Kellan didn't show up for our Introduction to Firefighting class. I had a feeling he was avoiding me.

"I know what your problem is," Travis claimed during lunch.

I swallowed my bite of chicken and lifted my gaze to meet his. "What's that?"

"You two don't know each other well enough," he said. "See, Laura and I were good together during testing, but the more we get to know each other, the better we work together."

"It's true," Laura said as she stabbed her salad with her fork. "It's the same with Caleb and Shaylene."

At the sound of their names, they both looked up. They'd been in their own little world, talking lowly to one another.

"We tried getting to know each other," I said. "Didn't work out so well."

"Have you tried hanging out with each other outside of class?" Travis asked.

"I mean, yeah… last night," I said, poking at my food.

"Yeah, but you were studying," he pointed out. "You need to get out of that environment."

"We were both at that party together." I was grasping at straws. That hadn't gone well, either.

"See?" Travis said. "That's good. You should get together like that more often."

Shaylene quickly piped up. "We're getting some people together in the Activities Center tonight. You should come. Bring Kellan."

I twisted up my nose. "Me? Play sports? With Kellan? That'll be fun."

"Yeah, it will," Laura said chipperly, ignoring my dry tone.

"Shit," Caleb said, checking his phone. "We're going to be late for class, babe."

Shaylene quickly stood beside Caleb. "I expect to see you there tonight, Cora. Gym C, six o'clock."

I faked a groan. "Do I have to?"

"You don't have a choice." Caleb winked at me, then grabbed his skateboard from under the table. The two hurried out of the dining hall side-by-side.

My eyes followed them as they passed the large windows, holding hands. I turned back to Laura and Travis once Caleb was out of sight. "What do I do if Kellan doesn't want to come?"

Laura shrugged. "Come anyway. It'll be fun."

I sighed and pulled out my phone to message Kellan. ***You busy tonight?***

You ready to talk? His text came only a minute later.

Ugh. He was so passive aggressive.

My fingers punched the screen quickly. ***Depends.***

On what?

Are you ready to be a decent human being?

I thought you knew. I'm not quite human.

I nearly snorted on my water I was drinking while I read the text. Laura and Travis gave me concerned looks, but I assured them I was fine and returned to my phone.

Fair enough, I texted. ***You up for a game?***

What kind of game?

Idk. Something in the Activities Center. My friends didn't say.

Do I have to be on your team? he asked.

I won't make you, I texted back.

Then I'm in.

"What are *you* smiling about?" Travis asked.

I slipped my phone in my pocket and returned my attention to my food. "Kellan agreed to join us."

"Ooh," Travis sang. "You *like* him."

My lips twisted in disgust. "Ew. Never say that again."

His features went blank. "What? What did I say?"

"Oh, Travis," Laura sighed. "You have so much to learn about women."

"Do I?" he teased. "I thought I was a pro."

Laura rolled her eyes. "Keep believing that."

By the time six o'clock rolled around, I was pumped. I spent most of my nights in my dorm room studying, so it was nice to get out for once. I dressed in a purple racerback tank top and a pair of black leggings, then followed Laura and Travis to the Activities Center.

The gymnasium was huge. A full track ran around the length of the room, and the ceiling was at least three stories tall. In the center of the track, endless foam pads had been set up. High above me, Davina and Aedes flew from one end of the gym to the other, performing aerial tricks and goofing off. It was mostly guys, and they were all shirtless. Large nets were attached to the walls on either end and secured high above my head to the level where people were flying.

Caleb swooped down from the air and tucked his white wings close to his back. He held a soccer ball and tossed it from one hand to the other. "You guys made it! Where's your partner, Cora?"

"I'm not sure," I admitted. "He said—"

"Right here!" Kellan jogged in through the doors and slowed beside us. He wore a tight blue t-shirt and didn't have his wings out.

"You're late," I joked.

Kellan looked out toward the middle of the gym, where Aedes and Davina were landing on mats and gathering together. He shrugged. "Looks like I'm right on time."

Kellan pulled his shirt over his head. Holy mother of God—those abs! He flexed his shoulders, and feathery midnight-black wings grew out of his back. I stared a little too long, then forced my gaze off of him.

Beside me, Travis had also stripped his shirt off and spread his white wings. He clapped his hands together and said, "Let's do this!"

"Okay, everyone gather round!" Caleb called.

There were around twenty people, and only two other girls besides Laura, Shaylene, and me. I knew about half of the guys from class, but the others I hadn't met before.

"Does everyone know how to play?" Caleb asked.

"I don't," a petite girl with jet-black hair said.

"This is what we call aerial soccer," Caleb explained. "It's a little soccer, a little football, but with a few modifications. For one, it takes place in the air." He gestured up to the nets on the wall that would serve as our goals. "Unlike regular soccer, you can touch the ball with your hands. The goal is to get the ball into the other team's net. Tackling is allowed, but the Activities Director has urged us to use caution, as we don't want to send anyone to the hospital with a broken wing."

"Eh, it'll be practice," Travis said with a shrug. "We'll get that patched up right here."

Caleb laughed. "If you screw up trying to heal me without a medical license, I'll sue you."

Travis's face paled, then he saluted Caleb. "No injuries tonight. Got it."

"We need team captains," Caleb said.

"I'll be one," Kellan offered, raising his hand.

"Cool. Anyone else?" Caleb asked.

"I will," I said quickly. Kellan didn't want me on his

team anyway. Might as well get on the other team as fast as I could.

Caleb stepped aside for me. "Kellan, you get first pick."

"I'll take Travis," he said without hesitation.

Travis beamed and moved to stand beside Kellan.

"Laura," I said.

"Sweet! I'm not last for once." She fist-bumped the air, then bounced over to stand beside me.

"Caleb," Kellan said.

"We'll take… Sorry, I forgot your name." I looked to a tall, athletic guy with black wings in my Introduction to Firefighting class.

"Miles," he said as he came to join Laura and me. He leaned over to her and whispered, "Your wings are sweet, by the way."

"Oh, these old things?" Laura joked.

We continued on choosing our teammates until we each had a team of ten. Shaylene looked pleased to be on Kellan's team with Caleb. Miles claimed the role of goalie, and the rest of us positioned ourselves in the air. Kellan and I faced each other as we hovered at the center of the gym. He shot me a challenging smirk.

"Ready?" Caleb asked from where he flew beside us.

"Ready as I'll ever be," I said.

"And… Go!" Caleb called. He tossed the ball between me and Kellan.

Kellan shot forward and reached out for the ball, but I kicked my foot at it instead. My toes connected with the ball, and it flew out of his grasp and toward Laura. She caught it and flew toward the goal, dodging out of the way of other players as she went. Kellan and I both shot toward her to stay on top of the ball.

"Over here!" a guy on my team named Everett called to Laura. Just before a girl on the other team swooped down to tackle Laura from above, she tossed the ball to Everett. He whacked it with his wing. It made a painful-sounding *smack*, but bounced into the net.

My team cheered. I stole a glance at Kellan, but he didn't seem bothered that we were already in the lead. He just looked like he was having fun.

The ball soared out into the middle of the gym after the other team's goalie kicked it. Kellan shot past me and caught it mid-air. He flew beneath one of my teammates, then shot back into the air once he passed them. I sped up to catch him, but before I could get there, he'd already handed off the ball to one of his teammates.

"Over here!" Kellan called just before his teammate was about to get tackled. He threw the ball back at Kellan.

I reached my hand out to stop it. It just barely grazed the ends of my fingers. Kellan caught it, then tossed it to another teammate, who took it all the way to the goal and shot it in before Miles could stop it.

"Tied game!" Caleb shouted.

Miles kicked the ball, and I quickly shifted course to follow it. I caught it, and Kellan's team started closing in on me at all angles. I twisted my body to dodge around one guy, then flapped my wings hard to shoot up and over Shaylene. I tucked my wings close to me and dropped several feet, then shot them out again to catch myself in the air as I dodged around another guy.

Then suddenly, something wrapped around my ankle, and I was falling. I let out a shriek and clutched on to the ball, flapping my wings harder to rip free. But it was evident my attacker wasn't going to let me go.

"Here!" a guy on my team named Tucker called.

I hurled the ball at him, but one of Kellan's teammates swooped in and caught it. My attacker let me free, and I finally saw that it was Kellan.

"Not fair," I said playfully.

"Hey, I don't make the rules," he replied innocently.

"Oh, so we're playing dirty now?" I laughed.

He shrugged, then continued on his way.

"Two can play at that game!" I called after him. I smiled as an evil plan began to form in my mind.

When the ball came toward him, I shot a white ball of essence in front of his face. It was the least powerful kind —the kind that would only stun him and wouldn't burn him—but it was enough to get him to twist out of the way. I swooped down and caught the ball he'd missed, then flew as fast as I could toward the goal. I threw it as hard as I could, and it soared past the goalie and into the net.

"Hey!" Kellan called. "Is that legal?"

I shrugged and hovered near the goal. "I don't make the rules."

"No stunning!" Caleb shouted. "It's a good way to break a wing."

"What if we're on the ground?" Kellan asked.

"Sure. Whatever," Caleb said. "Just don't stun anyone out of the air."

The game continued, and we were neck-and-neck the

entire way. I'd scored two more goals, but so had Kellan. I got ahold of the ball again, and almost instantly, someone's arms wrapped around my legs. I tossed the ball to my nearest teammate as fast as I could.

I took my eyes off the game as I tumbled toward the mats. I drew my wings into me until they disappeared, then rolled across the mats to catch my fall. I turned to see that Kellan had landed gracefully on the mats and was smiling in my direction.

I struck before he could. I shot a white glowing ball of essence out of my palm. He ducked, just barely missing it. It landed several yards beyond him and exploded like a firecracker. Kellan quickly shot his own essence back at me, though his was a dark color with a red center. I threw my body to the mat to avoid it.

"I don't think this is how the game's played," I told him.

"You keep scoring goals," he chuckled. "I gotta give my team a fighting chance to get ahead."

I threw another ball of essence at him, but he pulled his wings into himself and dodged out of the way. He quickly threw another ball at me, but I rolled out of the way to avoid it. It wasn't long before we were running around the mats and firing essence at each other in quick succession. Kellan kept coming closer and closer to me, and I was already out of breath.

"Can't we work out some sort of peace treaty?" I asked, just as I shot more essence at his head.

It whizzed just inches from his face, and his eyes went wide. "Try asking when you're not trying to knock me out."

I held my hands up in surrender, but he didn't give in.

He shot another ball of essence at me, and I jumped to avoid it. While my attention was on the essence, he sprinted forward and caught me by surprise. He grabbed me around the waist and tossed me over his shoulder.

"Hey!" I pounded my fists into his back, but he barely seemed to feel it. Instead, he spun us around on the mats until I got dizzy. I couldn't control my laughter. "This... is not... how the game... works."

He dropped me to the mat, then fell beside me, so close that we were almost touching. We were both out of breath and laughing. I turned my head in his direction and caught sight of his dimples. My laughter quickly died as I was reminded who I was goofing off with. Was this seriously the same Kellan I'd been having issues with all semester? It was so strange to see him in this new light—like we could actually get along.

Kellan caught my eye, but didn't lift his head off the mat. "What?" he asked innocently.

"I just... didn't know you were any fun." My cheeks flamed as I said it. I nudged him in the side, hoping he didn't notice my flushed face.

"Me?" he laughed. "I could say the same thing about you. Perhaps there's hope for you after all."

"Hope?" My eyebrows shot up. "You should be hoping I don't kick your ass in this game."

He looked up to the Aedes and Davina flying above us. "Eh, your team is doing fine without you."

Neither of us moved. It was silent on the ground for several seconds before I said, "I'm sorry about yesterday."

He waved it off. "Don't worry about it. We'll figure it out."

"You think?" I asked. "Because it feels like we do better when we're on opposite sides."

Kellan sighed, then pushed himself to his elbows. Hot damn. Those abs were still on full display. It'd be a sin not to admire them. He didn't seem to notice my eyes darting downward every now and then.

"Whether we like it or not, we're stuck with each other for now," he said. "So we're going to have to work as a team either way."

"Agreed," I said, sticking my hand out toward him. "Partners? Like, for real this time?"

He nodded, then shook my hand. A tingle of essence shot through me, and I knew he'd siphoned some just for fun. "Partners."

"Incoming!" someone shouted.

Kellan and I looked up to see essence raining down on us from all directions. He kept holding my hand and pulled me to my feet as we dodged out of the way. My heart lurched up into my throat, but the essence aimed at us had missed us. It all exploded into the mats, then disappeared.

"Attack!" someone shouted.

The players all landed on the ground, and our game of aerial soccer quickly turned into a game of essence dodge-ball. Somehow, the teams shifted—like we could all just sense where our loyalties lied. Kellan and I ended up defending each other. We ran over to Laura and Travis and formed a group as we dodged essence whizzing in all directions.

It was the most fun I'd had all semester. By the end of the night, I'd nearly forgotten how much I despised Kellan as my partner.

"Thanks for suggesting this," I told Shaylene as we left the Activities Center. "It was a lot of fun."

"And Kellan?" she asked. "Did it help?"

I contemplated it for a minute, but the answer was obvious. "Yeah. I think things might actually work out between us."

11

When I entered my Introduction to Firefighting class on Friday, something seemed different. I didn't realize what it was until I saw Kellan waving me over. He wasn't sitting in his usual spot. Instead, he was sitting next to the chair I normally sat in. We didn't have assigned seats, and most of the class so far had been lecture instead of practical application. When we worked with fire before, Kellan had avoided me, since I could work with any Aedes on my element and we only needed each other for our healing classes. But today, he seemed to think it was a good idea for us to pair up.

"Hey," I said as I sat. "What's up?"

"We're killing flames today," Kellan reminded me. "I thought it'd be good if we worked together, since we'll be up against this during our final."

"Good idea," I said.

Kellan eyed me. "You look kind of… unenthused."

I shrugged. "I'm just waiting for this class to get exciting, you know. I can't wait to dress up in firefighting gear and walk into a burning building."

Kellan chuckled. "We have a long semester left. But you have to learn how to kill flames first."

"I know how," I said confidently.

Kellan rubbed his hands together like an evil mastermind. "Well, I can't wait to see it."

I shook my head and rolled my eyes.

"Okay, everyone. Settle down," Professor Arnold said as he strolled into the room with Professor Taylor on his heels. The two were both middle-aged men and best friends, which made them perfect teaching partners. "Today, we'll be focusing on our Davina students and practicing killing flames. However, that doesn't mean that your Aedes partner doesn't have a very key purpose in this. Allow us to demonstrate."

Professor Arnold gestured for the class to come forward. We gathered around a large glass window that took up the entire wall. On the other side was an empty room made entirely out of fireproof materials. The only thing inside was a pile of firewood for fuel. We'd watched several demonstrations here before, but I could tell today was going to be good.

Professor Arnold turned to his teaching partner. "Professor Taylor, if you will."

"Yes, sir." Professor Taylor stood at a control panel and let out a maniacal laugh that made the class burst into laughter. The two played off each other and always made sure we were having fun in this class.

"Bombs away," Professor Taylor joked.

He pressed a button on the panel, and flames immediately ignited. They quickly engulfed the wood while Professor Arnold continued to speak.

"Over the past several weeks, we've covered the basics about firefighting," he said. "You know your equipment. You know your safety procedures. Now it's time to learn how to put your essence to good use in the field."

Professor Arnold turned back to the fire and aimed his palms to the glass. The flames instantly shrank, but they didn't completely disappear. "As you can see, I'm only capable of so much on my own. Professor Taylor?"

Professor Taylor came to stand beside him. He placed his hand on Professor Arnold's shoulder, drawing essence into him. I could tell the moment it happened, because the flames died quicker as Professor Arnold accessed more essence so he could perform more advanced magic. It seemed like only seconds before the flames died to embers, then the embers fizzled out to nothing.

"You see?" Professor Taylor said, turning back to the class. "This is why we continue to stress how important it is you get powered up before you go into a burning building, and why it's important you stick together. Your element will be stronger."

"Now, for the Davina in the class," Professor Arnold continued. "Don't get too hung up on extinguishing the flames completely today. All we want to see is that you're using the techniques from your Elemental Magic class and applying them to this setting. If you can't extinguish them fully today, you'll be able to by the end of the semester. I guarantee it."

"And if you can't," Professor Taylor cut in. "Good luck on the final."

The class shared a laugh, because we all knew what the final entailed. No way were any of us jumping into that without mastering this first.

"Are there any questions before we begin?" Professor Arnold asked.

Caleb raised his hand from the other side of the group, and our professor called on him. "So when we're actually extinguishing flames, are there any techniques to keep humans from noticing what we're doing?"

"Excellent question," Professor Arnold said. "We will be addressing those concerns another day. Right now, we want to master the art of our element before diving into that."

Shaylene's hand shot into the air next.

"Yes, Miss Hargrove?" Professor Arnold said.

"I'm just curious, why is it so important we keep our essence hidden from them?" she asked.

The question was innocent, but the entire room quieted. Professor Arnold shifted his weight between his feet.

"Coming out to the public has never ended well for us," he explained in a soft tone. "Humans greatly outnumber us. People are afraid of the unknown, and they react quickly and violently against the things they can't understand. We've kept our races secret for our own protection. At times when word has gotten out, we've been hurt for what we are."

"Hurt how?" Shaylene asked curiously.

Professor Arnold pressed his lips together, like the thought was uncomfortable for him. "A recent example involved a group of Aedes. It was around the time when their curse was broken and the Alliance was still working on assimilating the Aedes into our society. A group of humans caught some Aedes in their supernatural form. They called them spawns of Satan, captured them, and tortured them."

He didn't go into detail, but I'd heard the story before. They'd had their wings torn off and were beat to unconsciousness before the Alliance got word and made it there to save them. It wasn't the only time it'd happened, either. Of course, the Alliance kept it out of the media as much as they could.

"These past few years…" Professor Arnold trailed off, like there was something he wanted to say but couldn't. He had this faraway look in his eyes that made me shiver.

"Anyway…" Professor Arnold cleared his throat, cutting the tension in the room. "Back to our lesson. Who'd like to go first?"

A girl at the front shot her hand into the air. I would've half expected it to be Celina, had she been in this class. She was in the other time block, though, which I considered a blessing. I knew she'd show off if she had the chance—and she'd probably steal Kellan as her partner to do it.

Professor Arnold gestured her forward. "Pick a partner and step right up!"

The first team managed to reduce their flames by about half, but they couldn't get them down to embers.

"That's a great start!" Professor Taylor encouraged. "We'll make experts out of you by next week."

The next group was able to kill their flames to embers, but the wood still burned a hot red. When they pulled back their essence, the fire grew again.

"It's okay," Professor Arnold said. "You did great. Who's next?"

"We'll go," Kellan offered.

I froze. I'd wanted to watch a few more people before we went, but Kellan didn't seem to care.

"Come on up!" Professor Taylor said, like we were on a game show. "Show us what you've got."

Kellan and I made our way through the small group of students and stopped in front of the glass. He leaned over to quickly whisper to me. "We've got this."

"Thanks," I whispered back.

Professor Taylor pressed the control panel again, and the wood beyond the glass lit up in flames. We waited for Professor Arnold's signal, then Kellan placed his hand on my shoulder.

Essence flooded through me. I seemed to forget what it was like each time. That, or each time was more powerful than the last. I took a breath to steady my shaking hands, then held them up toward the glass.

"Remember that killing flames is different from creating them," Professor Arnold said to the class, though it felt as if he was reminding me. "You don't push your essence outward. You feel the essence all around you. You connect with your element and make it your own."

I concentrated on the flames in front of me. I tried to

picture them as my own, as those that would come shooting out of my palms if I commanded them to. I ordered the flames to die, but nothing happened. I didn't feel anything.

"Take your time," Professor Arnold said softly.

"Relax, Cora." Kellan squeezed my shoulder, as if letting me know he could feel the tension in it. I hadn't even realized it was there until he pointed it out.

I took a deep breath and did as he instructed. Then I felt it. A warmth spread across my hands, but it came inward instead of going outward. I pulled back on my essence, as if tugging on that might bring the flames into me and tone them down, but all that happened was that the warmth in my hands disappeared.

I suddenly felt very self-conscious. All eyes were on me, and I was taking longer than the other teams had. I glanced to Professor Arnold, and he looked to be analyzing me, like he could see my struggle.

"What are you feeling right now, Cora?" Professor Arnold asked.

"I felt my hands get warm for a second," I told him.

Professor Arnold nodded thoughtfully. "Good. That means you connected with the flames. But you must go beyond a simple connection and make them your own. Feel them as if they're your own essence, and then control it as you would the element that pours out of you."

I nodded and tried again. Kellan dropped his hand from my shoulder, since I didn't need the constant power-up for elemental magic as I did with healing magic. He stepped close to me and whispered under his breath. "You've got this, Cora."

I knew I could do it, but his encouragement meant a lot. I took another deep breath and let my essence flow around and around in my body, swirling instead of going out through my palms to make flames. I focused on the fire beyond the glass—and felt that heat again. I didn't pull back this time. I just let the heat come. Slowly, it crept over my skin, washing over me until it overtook my whole body and became one with the essence inside of me. When I could no longer tell the difference between the fire in front of me and what it felt like to conjure my own flames, I did as I would my own magic. I commanded it to die down. And like my own magic, it did. The flames went from licking three feet high in the air to nothing more than an inch.

"That's it," Professor Arnold encouraged. "Keep it going. You can do it, Cora!"

I commanded it further, and the small flames died out, becoming nothing more than lingering embers.

"You've got this, Cora!" Kellan sounded excited. "We're almost there."

I held my breath and pushed harder as the last few embers held on. I couldn't leave a single one behind. It wasn't acceptable in the field, which meant it wasn't acceptable in class.

Come on. Come on. Come on.

The last embers glowed a bright red, then instantly died. I breathed a sigh of relief as the class clapped for me.

"We did it!" Kellan cried.

"Excellent job!" Professor Arnold applauded. "You've done great. You two make a really great pair."

He clapped us on the back as another team stepped forward to give it a shot. Kellan and I stepped aside. I was still trying to wrap my head around what I'd done.

"Wow," I said. "I don't think I expected to get that on my first try. I mean, I've extinguished flames plenty of times, but they were my own, you know? Taking an existing element and *making* it mine was cool."

"Yeah," Kellan said. "I guess we really do work well together."

I held in a laugh and teased, "If you say so."

"Would you have done better with someone else?" He raised a challenging eyebrow.

I shrugged. "I don't know. But we still have a long way to go. Especially with healing."

"True," he agreed. "But this is a good start."

"I need an update," Laura said.

It was mid-October, and the trees around campus were beautiful shades of reds, oranges, and yellows. The sun was shining, but the air was chilly enough that I wore a thick sweater and a knit beanie. It was Saturday, and Laura and I decided to take the bus downtown to do some shopping. She wanted to buy a new pair of winter boots, and I wanted to go to an antique store that had just opened up. We'd asked Shaylene to come along, but she was busy with Caleb.

I shoved my hands into my pockets as we walked toward the front gates. "Update on what?"

She nudged me with her elbow. "Duh. You and Kellan. You've barely talked about him over the past few weeks."

I shrugged, but a slight smile touched my lips. "Things are better. Introduction to Firefighting is going great. Our connection makes my element stronger, which means I'm getting really good with my fire. But we could still use the extra practice with healing. He always claims he's busy when I suggest we study."

"What about in class?" she asked.

"I don't know," I admitted. "I thought we were doing better, but Professor Kovski seems disappointed in us. Which I don't get, because we healed those frogs last week just fine. We still barely passed the assignment, though."

"Mm…" Laura pressed her lips together in thought. "I don't know… Hey, how's your anatomy homework going?"

"Fine. Why?" I asked.

Laura shrugged. "I did great with the bones unit, but now that we're working on muscles, I'm having a hard time."

"We'll study together later," I promised.

We reached the front gates. The security officers gave a polite nod, then let us pass.

We walked the long stretch of sidewalk to the corner. When we reached the intersection, we both slowed. Down the wide sidewalk along the busy road, a group of at least twenty people were pacing the wall with picket signs that read things like *What are they hiding?* and *The truth will set you free!*

"Let us in! Let us in!" they chanted.

Next to them, two guys were fiddling with a remote control and bitching about how it wasn't working. When their eyes turned skyward, I noticed a drone buzzing high above our heads. The losers were trying to get footage of campus—and I was pretty sure the Alliance had some sort of device to jam their feed.

My eyes caught sight of another guy, and a chill traveled down my spine. He had blond hair and wore a blue blazer. It was the same guy I'd seen on my first day here, the pompous ass who tried to sneak onto campus.

I grabbed Laura's arm. "Let's cross the street."

She eyed the protesters, then said, "Good idea."

Before the light changed to let us cross, the group spotted us.

"Colt," a girl said to get their leader's attention. "There's some!"

Colt and three girls hurried over to us. I wanted to just ignore them, but they swarmed us on all sides.

"What are you hiding behind these walls?" Colt demanded. He was so close that he was practically touching me.

"Nothing," I insisted, stepping away from him.

"You're hiding something, or you'd let other people in!" His nostrils flared.

"Yeah," one of the girls sneered, getting up close to Laura. "Tell us what it is."

I saw the fear in Laura's eyes and threw myself between the two of them. "Seriously, lady. Back. Off."

"Not until you tell us—"

"Nothing," Laura snapped. "We're not hiding anything. It's just a private and sacred campus."

"If that's true, why can no one join your religion?" Colt snarled.

He was getting way too close for comfort. I was very conscious of the Davina Blade tucked into my boot and was seriously considering using it if it came to that.

"You're a cult," he accused. "You're hiding something!"

"Dude, take it up with the administration," I growled. "Leave us alone."

"Leave you alone!?" he roared. His face was starting to turn red, and spittle flew from his mouth. "You're one of them!"

I'd had enough. I was seriously starting to feel like they'd jump us at any moment, so I struck first.

"I said, leave us alone!" I shoved Colt, and he stumbled backward into a few other protestors who had made their way over to us.

His eyes widened in surprise, like he couldn't believe someone had the audacity to put their hands on him. He straightened up and pointed a finger at me. "She assaulted me! You all saw it."

"You came at me first!" I defended.

"What's your name?" he demanded. "I'll be filing a police report for this."

Good Lord. Was he serious?

I couldn't stand around and watch any more of this bullshit. The light changed, giving Laura and me the signal to cross. I took her hand, but we didn't make it a step off the sidewalk before one of the girls stepped in front of me to block my path. She was young like the rest of them, maybe only a few years older than me.

"You're not going anywhere until you answer the question," she demanded.

"Um, yeah, I am," I stated, stepping around her and pulling Laura after me.

Seeing she couldn't mess with me, she went for Laura

instead. She grabbed Laura's wrist and yanked her back onto the sidewalk.

"What the hell?" Laura shouted.

I shoved the other girl off her in an instant, and that's when it turned into a full-on brawl. Someone—I didn't see who—threw a fist at my face. My cheek throbbed in pain. Before I really knew what was going on, Colt had grabbed ahold of me and shoved me up against the wall surrounding campus. He leaned in to say something, but I didn't give him the chance. I shoved my knee up into his royal jewels, and he fell to the ground, clutching his groin.

I started to run over to Laura, but Colt reached out and grabbed my ankle. My body went tumbling, and my face smashed into a sharp rock on the sidewalk. Pain shot across my cheek, and I felt the warmth of my own blood running down my face.

"Let go of me, you freak!" I used my free leg to kick Colt's arm.

Just then, the sound of a horn honking cut through the screams. I looked up to see a black sedan rolling its passenger-side window down. I was surprised to see Kellan's face staring back at me from the driver's seat.

"Get in!" he shouted.

I scrambled to my feet and shoved two girls off Laura, who was fighting back fiercely. We jumped in the back seat of the car before anyone else could get their hands on us.

Kellan punched the gas, and we left the protestors in our wake. I finally breathed a sigh of relief. Laura lightly touched a tender bruise above her eye, and I clutched my cheek, which coated my hand in warm, sticky blood.

"Holy crap!" Kellan cried from up front. "What's wrong with you?"

"Wrong with me?" I asked in disbelief. "We're not the ones who started it."

His voice softened as he slowed the car at the next stoplight. "I'm sorry. I didn't mean that. It's just... you should know better than to get involved with people like that."

"Get involved?" I gaped at him. "We didn't mean to get involved in anything. We didn't know they'd be there or try to attack us!"

Kellan grabbed a handful of napkins from the front seat and shoved them at me. He looked concerned as his eyes traveled from my cheek to the blood on my hands. "Here. To stop the bleeding."

Kellan gently pressed on the gas when the light turned green. He turned down a quiet street. "All I meant is this group is kind of... crazy."

"Those are the protestors Kane Harris talked about during orientation, aren't they?" Laura asked.

"Yeah," Kellan said, holding tight to the wheel. "They call themselves the Infantry. And there are more of them."

I felt like I'd heard of them before but couldn't remember where. Then I remembered I'd briefly heard a group talking about them at the party we went to a few weeks ago.

"What's their deal?" I asked.

Kellan shrugged. "Don't know. They're just desperate to know what goes on inside the academy, I guess. Usually, they're harmless."

"Well, they're stepping up their game," I said. "I mean, they attacked us."

Kellan gritted his teeth. "I should turn around and—"

"No," I said quickly. "We don't need more trouble."

Kellan let out a heavy breath. "Fine. But we should tell Chancellor Harris."

"Do you think she can do anything about it?" I asked. "Like stop the protests or something?"

"Technically, the school can't do anything since they're protesting outside campus boundaries," Kellan said. "But she can report the incident. Maybe local law enforcement will actually do something about it."

"So it was a *good* thing they jumped us?" Laura asked.

"Depends on how you look at it," Kellan said, glancing back at us. "I'm sorry they hurt you. I really am."

"How'd you know they'd attack us?" I asked.

"I didn't," he said. "I went to pick up some pizzas for my study group since I'm the only one with a car, and I saw you on my way back."

"Study group?" I asked with a raised eyebrow.

He caught my expression in the mirror. "For… one of my other classes."

We made it back to campus, and the three of us showed our student IDs to the security guards before they let us through. Kellan parked the car, and we got out. Before I could start for the Academy Center, Kellan stopped me. He grabbed the napkins from me and took my face in his hand.

"Let me see," he said.

I held still, completely in shock at his touch. He stared

down at me and dabbed at the blood, but I barely felt the sting. All I could focus on was his warm fingers against the side of my face. I was acutely aware of his breath brushing across my skin as he inspected my wound, which wouldn't stop bleeding.

"Should we heal it?" I asked, mostly to break the silence. I couldn't tear my gaze from Kellan's face.

He shook his head. "Not yet. You'll want to show Chancellor Harris."

Kellan finally dropped his fingers, and I felt like I could breathe again.

"Are you okay, Laura?" I asked, turning to her.

She touched her bruise again. It was darkening by the minute. "Just a little shook up."

I had a feeling she was downplaying the pain. It looked bad.

We stopped outside Chancellor Harris's office, and Kellan explained to the receptionist what had happened.

"I'll let Chancellor Harris know right away," she said as she picked up her phone. "Please, take a seat."

We only waited a minute before the doors opened and Chancellor Harris invited us inside.

"I'll see you later," Kellan said with a wave.

"Wait," I blurted. He turned toward me expectantly, but I'd already forgotten what I was going to say. Instead, I said, "Thank you for your help."

He shot me a smile. "No problem."

I turned and followed behind Laura into Chancellor Harris's office.

"Please, girls," Chancellor Harris said. "Take a seat."

Laura and I sat in the two chairs in front of her desk. She took the seat behind it and folded her hands on the desktop in front of her. "I hear you had a run-in with the protestors outside campus."

"Yes." I quickly dove into the story of what happened.

Chancellor Harris looked more and more upset as the story went on.

"I can't believe anyone would protest the academy," I concluded with. "I mean, who could ever see us as a threat?"

Laura shrugged. "I mean, they don't know we're *not* a threat."

"I guess I get why we keep things a secret," I admitted.

"It's not really up for debate," Chancellor Harris pointed out. "It's our duty as supernaturals to keep our true nature secret."

"True," I agreed. "What can we do about this?"

"I think it's best if we report the incident to the police," Chancellor Harris said. "Perhaps then we can get these protestors off campus."

"Will it help, though?" Laura asked. "I mean, they could've done worse."

"Don't underplay it, Miss Blake," Chancellor Harris stated sympathetically. "What they did to you wasn't okay. You two were right to fight back. Will you be okay with filing written statements with the police?"

"Yes," the two of us answered simultaneously. We weren't going to let these assholes beat up any other students.

Chancellor Harris nodded. "I'll help you every step of

the way to get this reported. In the meantime, be careful when you leave campus. I would hate to see this group targeting the two of you."

"We'll be careful," I assured her.

Chancellor Harris picked up her phone and began dialing a number.

While she was preoccupied, I turned to Laura and whispered, "I'm glad Kellan showed up and got us out of there when he did."

"Agreed," she said. "I guess he's not such a bad partner after all, is he?"

My lips twitched at the corners. "No, I guess he's not."

I tossed and turned all night. I couldn't stop thinking about how Kellan had shown up out of the blue to help save us from those protestors. It was like he was a guardian angel himself—though I knew what he'd say to that if I ever accused him of it. I could hear his voice in my head. *I'm no angel, sweetheart.*

Don't ask me why dream-version of Kellan called me sweetheart. It was just his thing, okay?

When I woke the next morning, all I wanted to do was show Kellan how much I appreciated his small act of kindness. I brought it up to Laura and Shaylene while we were at the gym.

"Kellan doesn't seem like the kind of guy who takes thank yous well," Laura said as she bent into a squat. Her face looked better since we'd visited the health services center and gotten healed.

"No," I agreed. I picked up a fifteen-pound weight to

test it, then opted for the twenty-pounder. "I don't think he is. But I can't just do nothing, you know?"

"What should we do?" Laura asked. "Get him a gift basket or something?"

Shaylene snickered from beside her. With weights in her hands, she bent into a lunge and kept her eyes on the floor-to-ceiling mirror ahead. "Oh, Lord. Can you imagine that? What would Kellan do with a *gift basket*?"

"Good point," Laura said. "That idea is out."

Shaylene straightened, then switched legs. "If you really want him to know how much he matters to you, you have to make it personal."

"What?" I forced a laugh as I began curling the dumbbells. "Kellan does not *matter* to me."

Shaylene turned from the mirror and raised a skeptical eyebrow. "Let me rephrase. If you want him to know how much *what he did* matters to you… Do something that matters to him."

"Like what?" I asked.

Shaylene shrugged. "What does he like to do?"

I thought about it for a moment. "I don't know."

Laura sat on the bench press and took a swig of water. "Seriously, what do you two do when you're hanging out? Travis and I know practically everything about each other."

"Shaylene and Caleb don't talk either!" I defended. "They're too busy sucking face."

Shaylene threw her head back in laughter, then quickly said, "It's funny because it's true."

"At least Shaylene and Caleb interact like real people,"

Laura joked. "You can learn a lot about someone by the way they are in bed."

"Oh, God," I groaned, dropping my weights at my side. "Kellan and I are *not* getting into bed together. Besides, you're one to speak. You and Travis haven't even kissed yet."

"He hasn't made the move," she shot back playfully.

"Back to the topic at hand." Shaylene set her weights on the ground and came to stand by us. She stuck her hip out and said, "Doesn't Kellan have any hobbies or something?"

I shrugged. "I guess. He likes sports and fishing and stuff."

Laura wrinkled her nose. "I don't know if you can thank a guy with a fishing trip."

"I'll buy him a tackle box or something," I joked, but the sad part was it was the best idea we'd had yet.

Shaylene quickly shot the idea down. "Don't buy him a tackle box. In fact, don't buy him anything. If you really want to say thank you, give him an experience you want him to remember."

Laura wiggled her eyebrows suggestively.

"Ugh. Ew," I groaned. "Don't even joke about that."

I turned back to Shaylene. "You make a good point. I'll have to think about it."

It took me the rest of the morning and into the afternoon, but something Kellan had said weeks ago finally jumped out at me. I had an idea.

That afternoon, I knocked on his door, hoping he wasn't out. It swung open, and my jaw dropped. Kellan stood in nothing but a towel wrapped around his waist. His wet hair dripped water onto his muscled chest.

"You gonna stand there and gape at me all day?" he deadpanned.

I quickly shut my mouth and forced my gaze up to his face. "I, um, no…"

He stepped away from the door and gestured for me to come inside. "What's up?"

I hesitated a moment. I mean, the guy was naked and inviting me into his room. And it didn't sound like his roommate was around, either. My pulse quickened as I stepped inside. The door swung shut behind me, but I just stood there in the tight space between the closet and the bathroom, not stepping into the room fully. What was the protocol for being alone in a naked guy's room? I clutched the straps of my backpack tight in my hands.

Kellan reached into his dresser for a pair of jeans, then turned back to look at me. He raised a curious eyebrow. "Well…?"

"I was wondering if you wanted to go for a drive," I blurted.

"Am I the only guy you know with a car, or what?"

"Kind of," I admitted.

He pressed his lips together, like he was thinking hard. "Where are you planning to go?"

"It's a surprise," I told him.

Kellan stepped past me, and I had to push myself up against the closet door to let him through. His towel brushed against me, sending tingles up my body. He stepped into the bathroom and closed the door behind him.

"What kind of surprise?" he called through the door.

I smirked. He wasn't going to let this be easy. "The kind where you don't ask questions."

"Oh, that's how you're going to play it," he teased back. "So, this surprise… is it for me? Or are you just using me for my car?"

"I don't know," I said. "I guess you'll have to find out."

The door swung open, and Kellan stood there in all his gorgeousness. His jeans hung from his hips at just the right angle, and he didn't have a shirt on yet. His blond hair stuck up in every direction, which I thought actually made him hotter.

What the hell? I didn't find Kellan attractive!

"Well, are you intrigued or not?" I asked.

"A little," he admitted. He stepped back into the room and pulled a T-shirt out of his dresser. "But…"

"But what?" I asked. "Are you busy tonight?"

He hesitated. "No, not really."

"Then come with me," I begged. "I'll even pay for gas."

Kellan sighed. "Well, how can I argue with that?"

I bounced on my toes, beaming. "So, you'll come?"

"Will it help us as a team?" he asked, sitting down on the bed to pull on his socks.

"I hope so," I said truthfully.

"Then I guess I'm coming," he replied.

I smiled. "Awesome. I'm driving."

Kellan groaned. "Seriously?"

I shrugged. "It wouldn't exactly be a surprise if I told you where we were going, would it?"

Kellan frowned, but it was all in good fun. "Fair enough. Lead the way."

~

An hour later, I pulled down a long, secluded road with a line of trees on one side and a grassy field on the other. It was just outside of Eagle Valley, where I'd grown up. Almost no one came down here, except Aedes and Davina. No one else understood the significance of the landmark.

Kellan looked confused as we pulled into a small parking lot in the middle of nowhere. The sun was just setting, casting evening rays over the mounds of rocks in front of us. The rocks were out of place in the flat field, calling attention to the historic event that took place here twenty-five years ago. It was like a scar in the earth, marking the moment the realms nearly collapsed in on one another.

Kellan gaped, unable to take his eyes off the earth. "This is… this is the Malum portal site, isn't it?"

I nodded. "You said you hadn't had a chance to see it yet. I thought you'd like to."

Kellan's hand rested on his door handle, but he didn't open his door right away. "I didn't think you remembered."

"Hey," I joked. "I'm not totally heartless. I remember what my friends say to me."

Kellan finally tore his gaze from the mound of earth to look at me. "Are we friends?"

His question caught me off guard. I shrugged. "I don't know. Are we?"

He pressed his lips together in thought, but didn't answer.

I opened my door. "Let's go check it out."

I swung my backpack over my shoulder as we stepped out of the car and started for the portal site. Grass had overtaken the rocks over the years. Mom and Dad said that when the Malum portal collided with earth, a cavern had opened. When they'd destroyed the portal, the cavern came together to heal. It left behind this huge strip of heaved-up earth that overlooked the beautiful fields beyond.

Kellan and I climbed side-by-side to the top, using our hands to get over large boulders. By the time we reached the top, we were maybe only twenty feet up from the parking lot, but the site felt so significant that it seemed like we were on the top of the world.

Kellan took a seat on one of the boulders and looked out over the colorful landscape. The autumn leaves seemed to be every color of the rainbow. It was gorgeous.

I sat beside him. The boulder was big enough for two people, but small enough that we nearly touched.

"The actual portal opened up right there," I told Kellan, pointing to the end of the mound. "My parents said that you could see straight through it to the Aedes' realm."

Kellan shook his head lightly. "It's not our realm anymore. It hasn't been for a long time."

"I know," I said quickly.

Kellan turned to me. "Earth's our home, you know.

We've been here as long as the rest of you. It's just that now…"

He reached for a small rock beside himself and tossed it in his hands. "Now it's *really* our home, you know."

I nodded, but inside, my chest was twisting into knots. I didn't know what it was like for the Aedes. Before my parents destroyed the portal, the Aedes had been cursed, invisible to everyone but the Davina. Back then, the Davina hunted them. I wondered how much it still affected them—even Kellan, who never had to live through any of that.

His voice cut through the silence. "I know what you're thinking."

"Oh?" I asked, a little intrigued. "What's that?"

"You're wondering why I care, since I wasn't alive when any of it happened," he said.

I frowned. "Yeah, kind of."

He took a long breath, staring down at the rock in his hand. "It's not over, you know."

My brow furrowed. "What do you mean?"

He paused for a few moments, then said, "Your parents did a lot of good for our races in unifying them, but it's still a rocky ride for some of us."

"I get what you mean," I said softly. "We still have to hide ourselves from everyone else."

"I don't know that you *do* get it," Kellan said lightly. He wasn't accusing me of anything. It was more like he was stating fact.

I suddenly felt a sting in my chest. He looked kind of sad—vulnerable. It was strange, to say the least.

"Explain it to me, then," I offered.

He shook his head. "Nah, it's fine."

"I'm sorry that your parents had a tough time when their curse was broken," I said honestly. "Just because mine didn't doesn't mean I don't care. Help me understand. What was it like for your parents to go through that?"

Kellan hesitated, looking back over the landscape. "It wasn't my parents," he admitted. "Just my dad. My mom's human."

"Oh," I said flatly. "That's really uncommon."

I wanted to smack myself. That was all I had to offer? Seriously?

Fuck me. I was totally not offering any comfort. All I was doing was sticking my foot in my mouth. I did the only thing I could think to turn the moment around and changed the subject.

"I brought you something." I swung my backpack off my shoulder and set it on the rocks at my feet. I unzipped the zipper and pulled out a can of beer.

Kellan took it, and I noticed a slight hint of a smile cross his face.

"That's the kind you like, right?" I asked. It was the same kind he'd been drinking at the party.

"It's fine," he said, straightening up. He set the rock in his hand beside himself and popped open the top. He took a sip and smacked his lips. "Thanks. Where'd you get it?"

I smiled as he relaxed. "Bought it off Kumar. But wait; there's more."

His smile grew. "Is there?"

I reached back into the bag and pulled out two takeout containers of Pad Thai. I called upon my fire to warm it a little before I handed him one, along with a plastic fork. "You're okay with Thai food, right?"

"Yeah…" He sounded confused as he took the container from me. "I love it. How'd you know?"

I shrugged. "I saw an empty container in your room."

I reached back into my bag for one more item. "And if you're still hungry, I brought this."

I held up a bag of fresh-sliced deli ham. Kellan nearly choked on his beer.

"Oh my God," he chuckled once he finally swallowed. "Ham? Seriously?"

I smiled proudly, then placed it back in my bag.

Kellan rolled his eyes at me as he opened his take-out container. "I ate the ham, you know. The whole thing."

"Oh, I believe you," I said as I started digging into my own food. "Who can argue with free food?"

Kellan smiled. Silence settled over the portal site after that. All I heard was the gentle breeze brushing past us. It was kind of nice—serene. It wasn't until we finished eating and the last few rays of sunshine were fading that Kellan finally spoke.

"So, why'd you bring me here?" he asked. He'd set his beer and takeout container aside on the rocks and leaned back onto his hands. One arm kind of rested behind me, and I quickly became acutely aware of his proximity.

I blushed and turned away from him so he wouldn't see. "I wanted to thank you. For yesterday."

Kellan shook his head. "You don't have to thank me. I did what anyone would do when they see a girl getting beat up."

I finally turned to him with a raised eyebrow. "What *anyone* would do? Apparently that Colt asshole didn't get the memo—seeing as he was the one doing the beating."

Kellan pushed off the rock and sat up straight. His arm brushed against mine, sending tingles up and down the surface of my skin. "Yeah, well, guys like that are scum. He doesn't count."

I chuckled. "I don't know. I kind of think it's guys like you who are in the minority."

"Guys like me?" he asked.

I blushed even harder. What the heck was wrong with me today?

"You know," I said. "Nice guys?"

"Nice guys?" he repeated. "Is that a question?"

I shrugged. "I don't know. I guess the jury's still out on you. Sometimes you're nice, and sometimes you're a jerk. I haven't made up my mind which one you are yet."

A smile crept across Kellan's face. In the dying light, heavy shadows crossed his face, accenting his sharpest features. For some reason, I couldn't take my eyes off him.

"Maybe I'm both," he offered.

"Yeah, maybe," I agreed. "Or maybe you're one of the jerks and just saved me because you need me to pass the semester."

"That must be it." He bumped his shoulder into mine, and my whole body came alive with butterflies. He didn't seem to notice.

I laughed, mostly because I was starting to get uncomfortable with how my body was betraying me. I mean, I shouldn't be feeling this way. Especially not around Kellan. I had to be sick or something.

Kellan joined in on the laughter, but it was quiet, nothing more than a chuckle shared between the two of us. Then our eyes met, and we both went utterly silent. Our eyes locked, and we froze, like we were both waiting for the other person to say something. Without realizing it, my body inched closer and closer to his, as if magnetized. With each inch, my pulse increased, until my knees were shaking. I tilted my head up—

"Eh-hem." Kellan cleared his throat, breaking the spell between us.

We both jumped back from each other, like nothing had happened. My heart pounded violently against my rib cage, so hard that I wouldn't be surprised if Kellan could hear it. Had he felt the pull I'd felt? Did he even realize what was going on, that I would've kissed him if he let me?

The air suddenly felt heavier. Everything had quickly turned very awkward.

"It's, uh, getting dark," Kellan said. "We should probably get back to school. Early class in the morning."

"Yeah," I quickly agreed. I stood and reached for his trash. "I'll take that."

Kellan rose to his feet. He was so close to me that all I'd have to do is lean forward and we'd be pressed chest-to-chest. He looked down at me, but I couldn't read his expression.

"Thanks for bringing me here," he finally said.

I shrugged like it wasn't a big deal as we gathered our things. "Well, thanks for saving me yesterday. It was the least I could do."

But as we started on the drive back home, I couldn't help but think that maybe the night would've ended differently if I'd done more for him.

14

Several weeks passed, and Kellan hadn't mentioned the night in Eagle Valley to me again. I didn't know if it was because he didn't care or because he'd said all he could on the topic. I hadn't seen him since our Introduction to Firefighting class on Friday, since he wasn't in my Elemental Magic class that afternoon.

Laura and I were walking back to our dorms after lunch one Saturday when I caught sight of him in the distance. My pace slowed as my eyes followed him past the Winged Fountain. He was walking in a large group toward the Activities Center, with Celina at his side. My stomach felt hollow as he threw his head back in laughter at something Celina had said.

A sudden thought invaded my mind. He should be laughing at *me* like that.

Before I knew what was happening, my feet were carrying me in his direction.

Laura quickened her pace to follow me. "Where are you going?"

I pulled my jacket collar tighter around my neck to ward off the early November chill. There were flurries on the ground, though the snow wasn't sticking yet. "Um… I thought maybe we could go rock climbing?"

I couldn't tell her the truth—that some invisible force was pulling me toward Kellan. Half of me wanted to be with him at all times, and the other half of me was repulsed that the thought ever crossed my mind.

"Sounds like fun," Laura said. "Beats studying."

I kept my eyes on Kellan, and I was kicking myself the whole time. What was up with me? I was being a crazy, weird stalker. But turning back now would only make me look weirder.

When we got to the Activities Center, the entrance hallway was more crowded than usual. We noticed Travis and Caleb filling their water bottles at the drinking fountain. I finally tore my gaze off of Kellan as we made our way over to them. Kellan's group started in the opposite direction.

"What's going on?" Laura asked Travis.

He took a swig of water, then screwed the cap on his water bottle. "It's Grand Opening, babe."

Laura blushed a little when he called her *babe*. Those two needed to admit their feelings for each other already and make it official.

"Right," I said in realization. "The renovations on Gym B. We totally forgot."

Caleb turned away from the drinking fountain. "Exactly. Everyone wants a shot at it."

Laura bounced on her toes. "The obstacle course is finally open?"

Travis nodded and draped an arm around Laura's shoulder. "And it looks like we're partners."

Caleb groaned. "Come on, man. I thought we were going to dominate this thing together."

Laura giggled. "We can trade off."

Caleb scrunched his nose playfully, then his eyes caught someone else's in the distance. "I guess I'll partner up with Shaylene."

I faked a jaw-drop as he hurried off the meet up with her. "What about me?"

I heard someone sigh behind me, then a deep male voice said, "I need a partner."

I whirled around to see Kellan standing there. "How did you—?"

He was just ahead of me! Sneaky little bastard.

I eyed him skeptically. "I thought you'd team up with Celina."

"She's with Rhys," he said with a shrug. "Besides, the point of the course is to build up teamwork skills, and well… we're a team."

For some reason, my heart lifted in my chest when he said that. "O-okay. Teammates it is."

Kellan shot me a quick smile that sent my stomach somersaulting in my abdomen.

The four of us headed down the hall toward Gym B. We

came to a pair of double doors and entered a huge room bigger than a basketball court. Almost the entire thing was taken up by a horseshoe-shaped obstacle course, apart from the bleachers that were full of people. I kept my eyes on the course as we joined the line behind the sign-up table.

There were eight obstacles in total, all with tons of foam padding all around them. It seemed like half the school was here, with professors and teams roaming the gym. Over the loudspeaker, an announcer called teams up to the main platform. It looked like we'd already missed the opening ceremonies. Normally, the course wouldn't be so crowded, but the grand opening was kind of a big deal. They'd been building this course for months.

One team I didn't know was already working their way through the obstacles. They made it across a balance beam set over a large foam pit easily, thought it looked as if the beam was made to wobble beneath their feet.

The crowd cheered as we watched the team move on to the second obstacle. It was a set of monkey bars and looked easy to pass. The first team member jumped off a small trampoline at the platform below the bars. She got her hands around the first bar, but it spun on an axel, and she lost her grip. She tumbled downward with a scream and landed in the foam pit below her. A horn sounded, signaling the team's failure.

Ahead of us, Travis and Laura were discussing strategies. Kellan didn't say a word to me, so I scanned the gym, just for something to do. I spotted Celina and Rhys ahead of us, then glanced behind myself to see Caleb and Shaylene a few people back.

"Any ideas?" Kellan asked as the next team stepped to the first platform.

"Huh?" I asked, looking back to him. It felt strange to be standing here beside Kellan. Sure, we worked together in class all the time, but it was different being with him outside of class—since we weren't obligated. I wasn't sure why he'd even asked me to be on his team.

"Ideas," he repeated, gesturing toward the course. "Strategies?"

"Oh." I shrugged. "I was just going to wing it."

Kellan smirked, like he was amused. Was there ever a time this guy wasn't smirking? For whatever reason, I found it deadly attractive.

I quickly shot the thought down. What was wrong with me? Kellan wasn't attractive. He was still an asshole. Not as big of one as he was at the beginning of the semester, but an asshole nonetheless.

"Wing it?" he asked.

He eyed me skeptically, and I suddenly felt like I was being put under a microscope. I blushed and turned away to watch the team on the course. They wiped out on the third obstacle, one where there were three robes suspended in a row and you had to jump from one to the other to make it across.

"Hey..." Kellan nudged me with his elbow.

Heat pooled low in my belly. What was with my body today? It was like my element was going haywire or something. Plus, every time I looked at Kellan, all I saw was his face through the car window, offering safe haven from those crazy protestors.

"What's up?" he asked. "You're acting weird."

I shrugged and crossed my arms. "I don't know. I just… didn't expect you to ask me to be on your team."

Kellan stole a glance to Celina and Rhys ahead of us, who were laughing with one another. "Rules are rules. The obstacle course is for teams. I couldn't sign up alone."

"I thought you and Celina had a thing going on," I blurted. I wanted to quickly shove the words back in my mouth.

Kellan shifted his weight between his feet. "It's complicated."

Good. The thought came out of nowhere.

I breathed a sigh of relief when we reached the sign-up table and added our names to the sheet. We followed behind Travis and Laura to sit beside them on the bleachers, leaving some room beside us for Caleb and Shaylene.

I kept my eyes forward, studying the teams as they made their way through the course. For some reason, I couldn't look at Kellan. I felt like I had to keep my emotions under control around him, like if I looked him in the eyes, he'd read my mind or something. I watched the course as a Davina used his air magic to blow the ropes his way toward the platform he stood on so he could reach the first one.

Caleb and Shaylene joined us shortly after. None of us spoke until Celina and Rhys started the course.

"Bets?" Travis asked our group. "How far do you think they're going to make it?"

"I hope they fall off the balance beam," I mumbled. I

thought it was quiet enough that no one heard me, but Kellan started laughing.

"What?" I asked innocently. Meanwhile, Shaylene was betting they'd wipe out on obstacle number three, and Laura bet they'd make it to the end.

"Do you have something against Celina or something?" Kellan asked, like it was a shocker.

"No, of course not," I lied.

"Then maybe you should hang out with us sometime," Kellan offered. "You two would like each other."

I nearly choked on my own saliva. Was he serious? This girl had threatened me at the beginning of the semester. I didn't want to be *friends* with her.

But for whatever stupid reason, I found myself saying, "Yeah, sure. Sounds fun."

The team began the course. I held my breath as Celina ran across the balance beam. She was so quick that it seemed like her feet barely touched the beam. Rhys stood on the other side with one foot on the first platform and the other firmly on the beam, holding it steady for Celina. She made it safely to the other side, but I was still hoping to see her wipe out later. Rhys followed quickly behind her.

The two worked in sync to make it past the next five obstacles with incredible speed. They barely looked tuckered out. What the hell? The whole crowd was on their feet cheering for them as they neared the end, as they were the first team to get this far all day.

The seventh obstacle was a set of transparent walls with a foam pit between them. To get through, you had to tension your arms and legs between the walls to make it across. But when Rhys came up to the obstacle, it was clear that the walls were set too far apart for even him—and he was a huge guy. The two paused as their timer kept ticking away. We could see them talking from here, though we couldn't hear what they were saying. Finally, they parted and stepped up the wall.

The crowd went silent as we watched curiously. Celina and Rhys turned back-to-back and hooked their arms together. Each put one foot on either wall, then they pressed their backs together and put their next foot up.

"Holy crap," I said under my breath. "That's genius."

"It must be designed like that, so you can only get across as a team," Kellan replied.

Celina and Rhys inched across the length of the obstacle, using the tension of their teammate to keep themselves suspended above the pit. The further they made it, the more the crowd cheered.

Finally, they reached the other side, and the crowd erupted. People were on their feet, clapping and hollering as Celina and Rhys raced toward the last obstacle. The final obstacle was a rope net they had to climb to get to the buttons they pressed at the finish line. They seemed to scale the net at an inhuman pace.

They reached the top, and the crowd couldn't contain themselves. Together, Celina and Rhys pressed the buttons, and a loud buzzer sounded throughout the gym. Their timer stopped, and the announcer came over the speaker to recap their amazing run.

I clapped, because even though I didn't like Celina,

what they'd done was an incredible feat. I leaned over to Kellan and said, "If they can complete the course, we can, too."

He was also clapping, looking out toward the course at Celina while she waved to the crowd. "If we finish, that's good enough for me."

It wasn't long until Travis and Laura were up. Since Kellan and I were on deck, we stepped up to the starting platform behind them. We cheered as they began the course.

Travis and Laura held on to each other as they passed the balance beam, using each other as an anchor until they made it to the other side. Travis let Laura go first on the monkey bars. It looked like she was about to slip off, but she grabbed the next bar quickly and caught herself. It seemed like some of the bars rotated while others were stationary, and you had to figure out which ones to grab.

The two made it through the ropes next, then came up on the fourth task. Only a couple of teams had made it this far today. A timer high up on the ceiling counted the seconds they'd been on the course. So far, they had the best time, even better than Celina and Rhys.

The fourth task was a series of swinging steps. They were like the swings we'd played on as kids, only with hard bases for your feet. Laura nearly fell into the foam pit as the swing behind her slipped beneath her feet, but she caught herself on the ropes that held the swings up. Travis was behind her in an instant, helping her back up onto the swing.

I breathed a sigh of relief. "Only four more to go. I think they could make it!"

The fifth obstacle was a tall wall set at a steep incline that you had to run up to get onto the platform at the top. It was practically a ninety-degree angle and over a dozen feet tall, with a curve at the bottom that reminded me of the ramps at a skate park. The rules said you couldn't use your wings and that you only got three tries. Laura gave it a shot twice, but she couldn't get herself high enough to reach the platform. Travis said something to her, though we couldn't hear it. She backed away, and he took a running start at it. His fingers reached the platform, but they slipped before he could pull himself up. His second attempt yielded the same result, as did his third.

The buzzer rang, signaling that the team had failed. They didn't look disappointed, though. If anything, they looked like they'd had a lot of fun. The two stepped off the course smiling and laughing with one another. Then, in front of everyone, Travis leaned down and planted a kiss right on Laura's lips. She seemed shocked at first, until she brought her hands up behind his neck and kissed him back.

My jaw dropped, but I was beaming. I was happy for them.

"We're up next," Kellan said, pulling my attention away from the couple. "Mind if I power up?"

I shook my head, and Kellan placed his hand on my shoulder, drawing my essence into himself. Color filled his cheeks, and he looked energized.

He gestured to the balance beam in front of me. "Ladies first."

I took a deep breath and fixed my eye on the course. I knew this was all just fun and games—a training exercise— but I didn't want to be the girl who wiped out on the first obstacle. I glanced back to Kellan for a moment, but my gaze traveled beyond him. I caught Celina's eyes in the crowd. She stared me down, wearing a challenging smirk on her face. It was in that moment that a stone-cold resolve came over me. I was going to beat Celina's time and shove it in her face.

I slammed my hand down on the button at the beginning of the course, which started our time on the clock. I began across the beam quickly, but it wobbled so much that I had to slow down. I held my wings out at the sides to help me balance as I inched across to the other side.

You're going too slow, one voice in my head chastised.

Slow and steady wins the race, I shot back at myself. It was better to get across slowly than not at all.

I reached the other side, and Kellan started across the beam himself. At some point when I'd been walking across, Kellan had ditched his shirt. His black wings were at his sides, steadying himself. I hesitated a moment. He was moving much faster than I was, so I turned to the next obstacle to get ahead of him so I wouldn't slow him down.

I pulled my wings into me, then bounced off the trampoline to the monkey bars. Instead of going for the rotating spokes, I held on to the thick support bars on the sides. My body swung side to side as I moved my hands forward, until I was over the next foam platform. I gave my body one final forward swing, then jumped down onto the safety of the platform. I turned to see Kellan was using my same strategy and was close behind.

The next obstacle was the ropes. The first was close enough to reach, so I grabbed as high as I could and kicked off. I reached for the second rope and caught it, but I didn't let go of the first soon enough. I swung backward with both ropes in my hands, until I was at a standstill between the two of them. I didn't give myself too much time to hesitate. I dropped my feet from the first rope and twisted them around the second. I went swinging toward rope number three and caught it without a problem. At the peak of my swing, I let go and went flying toward the next platform. I landed with a hard thud and rolled across the foam to catch my fall.

By now, my arms were aching, and I was breathing heavily. But I was no stranger to heavy physical activity, since I had to train for firefighting. I knew I could do this.

I shook my shoulders out and eyed the sharp incline in front of me. I took a running start and jumped up the wall. My fingers just barely touched the platform, but they slipped. I went tumbling down the wall and rolled to keep from twisting an ankle. I heard the crowd react, but I tried to block it out. It'd only distract me.

Kellan had caught up to me. While he took a momentary break, I turned back to the wall and prepared to tackle it again.

"Wait," Kellan said quickly, stopping me. "We each only get three tries. Let me give it a go."

Was that a challenge?

"As you wish." I stepped aside.

He ran up the wall, giving one last thrust upward at the peak of the incline. His fingers curled around the platform, and his muscles rippled as he pulled himself upward. The crowd cheered, and I went breathless as he stared down at me with a proud smile on his face. He bent to one knee and held an inviting hand out.

I grumbled. If he helped me, it'd make me look weak. I wanted to do this on my own.

I backed up and ran up the wall again. Instead of reaching for his outstretched hand, I went for the bottom of the platform as he had, but my fingers slipped again, and I tumbled back toward the ground.

"Come on, Cora," Kellan's smooth voice said from above me. He kept his hand out toward me as I righted myself again. "Let me help you."

"It makes me look weak," I said up to him.

He frowned. "This is a team course, Cora. The only weakness you can show is not letting me help you."

I stood at the base of the wall for several seconds, trying to catch my breath. Above us, the clock continued to tick, counting our time. We were quickly reaching Celina's time.

"Do you want to get up this wall or not?" Kellan asked. I could see the challenge in his eyes.

Shit. He was right. I only had one shot left, and I didn't have the strength or the height to do it on my own.

Sighing, I backed up and ran toward Kellan. My left hand curled around the platform, while my right caught his hand. Electricity shot between us when we touched, but he didn't seem to notice. He pulled me upward, until I hooked my foot on the platform and pulled myself the rest of the way. I stood beside him, catching my breath.

"See?" he said. "A little teamwork goes a long way."

I rolled my eyes and punched him playfully in the shoulder. "Yeah, yeah. You were right. Next obstacle?"

To get to the next platform, we had to use our wings to glide down. Kellan and I flexed our shoulders at the same time, and our wings shot out on either side of us. Mine smacked into his, and he went stumbling forward. Before I knew what was happening, Kellan's foot slipped off the edge of the platform. My heart sprang into my throat as he went tumbling down to the mats below us. He landed with a loud *thud,* and a *crack* sounded across the gymnasium.

The crowd gasped and rose to their feet as Kellan rolled on the ground, spewing a sling of curse words.

"Oh my God!" I cried.

I flung myself off the platform and spread my wings out wide, soaring down to him. A knot formed in my chest as I knelt to his side.

"Kellan…" I reached out to touch him, but he curled in on himself, shying away. His wing was twisted in the wrong direction, sending my stomach plummeting to my toes. My own wings ached at the sight. "Oh, God. I'm so sorry. Can I heal you?"

Kellan cradled his wing into himself but didn't say anything. I felt completely hopeless. Travis and Laura rushed over to us and knelt beside Kellan.

"Dude, are you okay?" Travis asked, inspecting the broken wing.

"Do I look fucking okay?" Kellan growled through gritted teeth.

"It's fine," Laura said softly, trying to be the comforting friend she was. "We'll heal you—"

She was cut off as Professor Kovski and Professor Sanders arrived. "Move aside," Professor Kovski commanded.

Travis and Laura stepped back just as Caleb and Shaylene arrived. Celina abandoned Rhys and shoved her way over to us. She practically knocked me over as she dropped to her knees beside Kellan. She took his hand in hers, and he squeezed it back.

"I'm here, babe," she said in a voice that made me want to hurl. It sounded so fake.

"Everyone back!" Professor Kovski barked.

It was like I was watching myself from above as I rose to my feet and took a step back. I was still in an utter state of shock. Broken limbs and bloody wounds I could handle. I was going into the medical field, after all. But watching Kellan squirm in pain was entirely different. It made my stomach twist into knots and sent a lump forming in my throat. My eyes welled up for him.

"Kellan, I'm sorry," I said, but he didn't seem to hear me as Professor Kovski inspected his twisted wing.

"It's definitely broken," she announced. "You'll need to keep your wings out while we heal it, Mister Greene. If you shift, you could do more damage the next time you bring them out."

Kellan squeezed his eyes shut and gritted his teeth. He still hung on to Celina's hand, like he needed her to get through this. I suddenly had the thought that *I* should be the one holding his hand.

"I'll do whatever you say," Kellan said. "Just heal me."

Professor Kovski frowned. "I'm afraid it's not that simple, Mister Greene. We have to set the bone before we can transfer our essence, or it will heal wrong."

He knew that. It'd been discussed in class plenty of times. But he didn't look like he was thinking straight. His face had paled, and sweat had broken out on his forehead. He'd gone into shock.

Two professors I didn't know ran over with a stretcher and a first-aid kit. Everything happened so fast. They hoisted Kellan onto the stretcher, with his wings hanging limply at his sides.

"Miss," one of them said to Celina, who was still holding Kellan's hand. "I'm going to have to ask you to step back."

"No," Kellan said weakly. "She's good."

My chest twisted into a tight knot.

They let Celina walk with him as they rushed him out of the room and toward the health services center on campus. I found my feet moving under myself before I made the conscious decision to follow. I rushed up alongside Kellan.

"Kellan," I said breathlessly. "I'm so sorry. It was an accident."

"Miss, please," one of the professors begged. They paused at the gym doors as several onlookers rushed to hold them open for the stretcher.

Kellan took the moment to open his eyes and look up at

me. For a moment, the deep blue of his eyes melted my heart, and then he opened his mouth—and shot a dagger straight through me. "Every time I think you've made progress, you turn around and show me just how wrong I am."

That was all he said before he was rushed out of the room. I remained firmly planted in place, staring after him as his words sunk in. The knot in my chest tightened, until it felt as if I was suffocating.

Laura came up beside me and touched my wing to get my attention. "He'll be okay, Cora."

I swallowed hard and turned to her, blinking away the tears. "I know, but..."

She caught the horrified look on my face. "But what? What'd he say to you?"

I shook my head, trying to get the words out of my mind. "Nothing," I lied. "I just... I think I broke more than his wing... I think I broke our trust."

15

I wanted to see how Kellan was doing, so I texted him and asked him to tell me when he was healed. Hours passed, and his reply never came. I was starting to get worried, so I visited his dorm room to make sure he was okay. His roommate, Warner, answered and told me Kellan wasn't around. Worry tightened in my stomach. I texted Kellan again.

Did everything heal okay?

No response.

I knew it was only a broken wing, but my anxiety kept telling me there were complications that killed him or something. Yeah, it was over the top, but what else was I supposed to think?

I went to the health services center, and the receptionist there told me he'd been released over an hour ago. That jerk! I was seriously worried about him. Without any other options, I returned to our dorm hall and sat outside his room, waiting for him to return.

While I waited, I played with my element. Fire danced around in my palm, warming up my skin. I played with controlling the angles of the flames, trying to get an image to form like I'd seen Celina do on move-in day. I'd been working on it all semester. The best I could do was sustain the figure of a kitten in my palm, but as soon as I tried to add motion, my flames became unstable.

It was an hour before Kellan showed up. He noticed me as soon as he entered the hallway. His step slowed, but he approached me anyway.

"What do you want, Cora?" He barely looked at me as he made a beeline for his door.

I quickly stood. "I wanted to apologize. I feel awful."

Kellan paused with his hand on the door handle. "Good. You should."

My jaw dropped at his tone. "What the hell?" I snapped.

Kellan opened the door, barely acknowledging me. He left it open behind him, but didn't invite me in.

I crossed my arms in the doorway. "Are you really going to act like this?"

He turned to me. "Act like what?"

"Like... like..." I couldn't find the words. "Like *you*."

Kellan scoffed, but it was more like my choice of words amused him than upset him. "Sorry, sweetheart. It's who I am. Take it or leave it."

Holy crap! He actually called me *sweetheart*. What the heck was up with that?

Warner looked uncomfortable and started toward the door. "I'm just gonna..."

He didn't finish his sentence as he stepped past me, gesturing for me to step inside.

I took the invitation and let the door swing shut behind me, leaving Kellan and me in privacy.

"I just mean…" I started. "I came to apologize, and you're kind of being a jerk about it."

He plopped down on the bed, not even looking at me. It was like he *wanted* to prove my accusation.

I moved to the foot of his bed, where he couldn't ignore me. "It was an accident, Kellan. Why are you so mad at me?"

He crossed his arms and looked to the mural on his wall.

"Besides that, why didn't you answer my texts?" I demanded. "I was worried. You let me think something bad had happened to you. And when I went to the health services center, you weren't there."

His gaze darted to mine. "Oh, so you're stalking me now?"

"No!" I pressed my fingers to my eyes. "God, what is going on, Kellan?"

He sat up in bed and looked straight at me. "I get that it was an accident, Cora, but it was more than that. We were supposed to be working as a team. You hurt me because you'd rather do things on your own than work with me to get ahead."

My stomach sank. There was something in his tone that suggested I'd hurt him in more ways than one. My knees suddenly felt weak, so I sank into the chair beside his desk. "I'm sorry, Kellan," I whispered. "I didn't think—"

"Exactly," he cut in. "You didn't think."

"Seriously?" I snapped. "You're going to call me stupid now? I won't put up with that shit from my partner."

"So request another one," he insisted. "I've been putting up with your shit all semester."

"What shit?" I demanded. It was like he was grasping at anything he could to get angrier at me.

"You're not a team player," Kellan accused. "And you keep proving to me that that'll never change."

A lump formed in my throat. "How am I supposed to be a team player with someone who doesn't want to be on my team in the first place?"

"I *do!*" Kellan practically shouted. "I'm the one who asked you to team up with me on that obstacle course. Yet you still think I'm the same guy you started the semester with. A lot has changed since then."

It was hard to see it when he was acting like the first week I'd met him.

"So, what?" I asked softly. "Do you want to quit being my partner? We've worked so hard."

Kellan clenched his jaw, considering the question. Instead of answering, he said, "Can I ask you something?"

I hesitated, not sure where he was going with this. "Sure."

Kellan's tone softened. "What do you think of me?"

The question caught me off guard. What *did* I think of Kellan? It sounded like a trick question. I went with the easy answer.

"I think you're kind of a jerk." It wasn't anything he didn't already know.

Kellan looked like he wanted to smile but was holding back. "Guilty. But no, I mean…"

He paused. "What do you want? From me, as your partner?"

"I don't know," I admitted. "I just want to finish what we started and get through the semester."

Kellan's shoulders fell, like it wasn't the answer he was looking for. He lay back down in bed and turned on his side toward his wall. "Apology accepted. You can go now."

Except it didn't sound like he accepted it at all. He seemed very hurt.

"Kellan," I said softly, feeling the weight of his rejection in my guts. "I really, *really* am sorry. What can I do to make this up to you?"

He shook his head, like there was nothing I could do. It wasn't even about the broken wing—that could be healed. It was about something bigger, something I didn't really understand and couldn't wrap my head around.

"Please talk to me," I begged. "I want to understand."

"I think we're both on the same page," he grumbled. "By the end of the semester, we'll change partners, like we agreed."

My jaw dropped. It felt as if he'd shoved a dagger into my stomach and twisted it around.

He didn't seem to notice. "I'll see you Monday in class."

It was clear there was no wiggle room with him. He wasn't going to give me any more than he already had. Though I didn't want to leave him, I stood and made my way toward the door. It seemed like that was what he wanted right now.

And that was all I could give him.

Over the next few weeks, Kellan and I didn't talk much. We just kind of went back to being lab partners—nothing more. When I tried to talk to him and get him to open up, he barely humored me with a response.

At least I didn't have to work with him in my Elemental Magic class. It was the one class we didn't have together.

"Today, we'll be shaping our elements," Professor Swan announced one day in class. She was an older woman, who had been studying elemental magic since the Davina discovered it. "The more you learn to control your element in the classroom, the more control you will have over it in the field. Celina, would you help me a moment?"

Celina stood proudly and walked to the front of the room. Our class was small, only about thirty people, and entirely Davina—all except Laura, who was half Aedes, half Davina.

"Celina, can you demonstrate creating and sustaining a fire tornado?" Professor Swan asked.

"Can I get a power-up?" Celina asked.

Professor Swan stepped aside. Her teaching partner, Professor Roberts, who was a younger Aedes woman, pulled Celina's essence into herself to open up her magical channel.

Celina took a refreshing breath. She didn't say anything before she started swirling her hands in front of her. Fire seemed to grow out of her palms like vines, each stream wrapping around one another until they formed a large funnel that hovered only an inch above the tile.

"Excellent!" Professor Swan praised.

I sat back in my chair, observing closely. I could create and sustain fire tornados, too. What was the big deal?

"Now, create a scene for us," Professor Swan instructed.

Celina smirked proudly as her fire tornado split into two, then settled down until the tornados transformed into two human figures. They looked like flaming marionettes as she twisted her hands to control them. One figure was clearly a woman, and the other a man. The woman twirled and danced around the man while he watched in admiration. As the woman slowed, the man got to one knee and held up a flower. A fricken flower! How'd she get that kind of detail? It was insane.

The fire girl shied away, then continued dancing, while the man continued to hold the flower up to her. When she didn't respond, he put the flower in his pocket and got to his feet. The woman stopped dancing and came running toward him, pressing a kiss to his lips as he pulled her into an embrace.

The story looked like it was going to continue, but Professor Swan cut Celina off. "Very well done!"

"Thank you." Celina smiled proudly.

The class applauded as Celina returned to her seat. I joined in, but I was still dumbstruck as to how she'd worked in so much detail to her flames.

"That was amazing," Laura leaned over to me and whispered.

"Yeah," I said flatly. "I don't know how she did it."

Laura shrugged. "I guess she's just really good."

"Each of you will be shaping your element like this today," Professor Swan said. "We'll be going around to your tables to observe. You're free to take any props you'd like from the table up front."

She gestured behind her, where rocks sat for earth Davina, along with vials of colored smoke for air and water bottles for water.

"If you need a power-up, please raise your hand," Professor Roberts offered.

Almost half the class raised their hands, and she started her way around to open their essence channels.

Laura turned to me. "Do you need a power-up? I can help."

"Yeah, that'd be great."

When Laura channeled my essence, it wasn't nearly as strong as when Kellan did it. It wasn't enough to heal, but it'd let me conjure fire for a day or two.

"Thanks," I told her as I held my hands up and summoned flames.

"I'll be right back," she said. She bounced up to the front

table and came back with a bowl full of pebbles.

"That's pretty cool," Laura said, eyeing the bird I'd made in my palm. It hovered there like a mere silhouette. I couldn't get the details in the feathers.

"Thanks," I said. "What can you do?"

Laura held her hands over the bowl. "I could use a power-up, but we'll see what kind of juice I have left over from our last class."

Laura twisted her fingers, and pebbles rose out of the bowl, creating a corkscrew spiral. When she tried to expand them into another shape, they shuddered in the air, then rained down onto the table.

"Crap," she mumbled, diving for the few that had bounced off the table.

"No, it was good," I assured her.

She gathered her pebbles back into the bowl. "Can you make the eagle fly?"

"Oh, um…" I looked back to the flaming eagle I'd made. "I don't know. I'm still trying to work out the details in it."

Laura looked thoughtful. "Maybe try animating it first, then adding the details later. It might be easier."

I wasn't sure, but I decided to give it a shot. "Okay."

I commanded my essence to move to the rhythm of flapping wings. But instead of making just the wings move, the entire figure bobbed up and down above my palm.

"Good start, Cora," Professor Swan said.

I hadn't noticed her approach. I got a little startled, and my fire fizzled out. "Um, thanks."

"Your control is very good," Professor Swan told me. "I really enjoyed the figure you created. But when you animate your essence, you must focus on each moving part as a separate piece to a larger puzzle—just as if you were controlling a large fire, you would begin by extinguishing it in sections rather than trying to do it all at once."

"That makes sense," I said. "Thanks for the tip."

Professor Swan nodded, then moved on to the next table. I glanced around to see that several of the other fire Davina were having trouble shaping their essence into anything but a sphere. One water Davina had created a mass of water that defied gravity. It hovered above his table and fell like raindrops onto the surface. Beside him, an air Davina creating a purple smoke swirl, then directed his air through the raindrops, dodging them as they fell.

Professor Roberts came to our table a moment later. "Do either of you need a power up?"

"Yes," Laura said. "I do."

Once her essence channel was open, Laura was able to control the pebbles with such finesse that she created a sculpture of a cat and made it walk across the desk. It sat in front of me and started licking its butt.

I broke out into laughter and couldn't focus on my element. "Oh my God, Laura. Seriously?"

She couldn't contain her laughter. "You think *that's* funny?"

Laura twisted her fingers, and the rocks moved to her command. They rearranged themselves into a very crude sculpture that made even cruder movements.

"Laura!" I cried.

She died of laughter, and her rocks went scattering across the table. "Your reaction makes it worth it."

I caught Celina glancing our way. She looked at us like we were a bunch of freaks.

Laura finally composed herself. "Okay, I'll behave myself. Let's see you try again."

I took a deep breath. "I'll *try*."

Celina had finally looked away, thank God.

I formed the eagle in my palm again. This time, I focused on keeping the body in place and only giving motion to the wings. To my surprise, Professor Swan's advice worked immediately. The eagle animated and began flying around the table.

Laura clapped and cried, "Awesome job, Cora!"

Celina shot another glance our way. I held my head up proudly as my tiny fire eagle soared above my head. She looked less than pleased.

I ignored her and turned back to Laura. "Look at us. We work well together. I don't know why *you* can't be my Art of Healing partner."

Laura sighed. "Because our essence isn't compatible for it. Plus, I like being Travis's partner."

I wiggled my eyebrows suggestively. "In more ways than one."

She giggled, but didn't deny it. "I don't get how you and Kellan can be so compatible with healing magic but like, not in actual life."

I shrugged. I didn't get it either. "Maybe we're too similar and that's why we butt heads. I seriously just want to get through this semester and change partners."

Laura frowned. "Are you sure? I mean, will being with

someone else make things easier, or do you think you and Kellan can work things out?"

"I don't know," I admitted. "Even if I stick with him through school, it doesn't mean we'll be together in the field forever. It might be good to give it a shot with someone else."

"Don't make any fast decisions," she warned.

I chuckled. "Fast decisions? This thing with Kellan has been going on for months."

"Exactly," Laura said. "And you've worked so hard. And I can tell—"

She cut off.

"You can tell…?" I pressed.

She sighed. "I can tell you guys enjoy working together when you try."

I raised my eyebrows. "I doubt it. Besides, he already made his decision. He's going to request a reassignment before next semester."

She frowned. "Maybe you can change his mind."

If only.

"Take the Thanksgiving break this weekend to think it over," she suggested.

I wasn't feeling confident about that, but I answered anyway. "Yeah, okay. I will."

I only said it to end the conversation. For some reason, I was starting to get uncomfortable with it. But as I considered what she said, I realized I really didn't know what I wanted. Did I want to fight to stay Kellan's partner or opt for a new one?

I guess I had a long holiday break to decide.

17

Dad picked me up from school Wednesday night, and we drove home in silence. He tried to get me to talk, but I didn't know what to say. That I'm having guy troubles? I could see that going down so well. Dad would drive straight to the academy with his police cruiser and gun on his hip to give Kellan a piece of his mind. So I just gave him the standard answers and told him things were going great.

When we arrived home, Mom had just returned from the restaurant. She was still climbing out of her car, and her face lit up when she saw our headlights pull into the driveway. We lived on a two-acre wooded lot just outside of Eagle Valley. Our house was two stories, with brown siding and stone accents.

"Cora!" Mom squealed, rushing over to the passenger side as Dad parked the car.

I flung open my door and rushed into her arms. She

squeezed me tightly, and I inhaled the fresh scent of her lavender shampoo. "Mom! I missed you."

She gave me one last squeeze, then drew away. "We missed you, too."

"Well, if you bought me a car, I could come home more often," I teased.

"In your dreams," she joked back. "Here. Let me help you with your bags."

"I don't need any help," I told her as I reached into the back to grab my backpack. It was all I had, since I was only staying for the four-day break.

"Oh, okay…" Mom looked a little flustered, like she was disappointed I wouldn't be staying longer. "In that case, I brought some leftovers home from the restaurant. Can you help me with them?"

"I've got it," Dad said quickly. He hurried over to her car to grab a stack of pies out of the back. There must've been at least five of them.

"Holy crap!" I said. "Are we hosting the whole town for Thanksgiving?"

Mom laughed as we started for the door. "Not unless you invited them. It's just going to be us three."

"What about Grandma Gloria?" I asked.

"She and Calvin are spending Thanksgiving on a cruise," Mom explained.

"What?" I squeaked. I paused to hold the front door open for Dad. "She didn't tell me."

"She's too busy having fun," Dad joked.

We stepped inside, and the smell of home hit my nose. I didn't even know our house had a smell until I'd spent time away. The scent of cinnamon candles and fresh linen was an instant comfort. Kellan quickly fell to the back of my mind as I stepped back into my old life. A huge TV sat across from the brown leather couches, with a stone fireplace set into the wall between them.

"Do you want these in the kitchen?" Dad asked Mom, gesturing to the pies he was carrying.

Mom rolled her eyes. "No, I want them in the garage. Yes, I want them in the kitchen."

Dad disappeared down the hallway, and Mom turned to me. "Sit down, Cora. Tell me all about how school's going."

"I'm actually really tired," I admitted. "Can we talk tomorrow?"

She frowned. "Okay. Are you going to help me cook? I'm making your favorite: honey glazed ham."

I laughed, but Mom just looked confused. "It's nothing," I told her. "My partner and I just kind of have an inside joke about ham."

Her brow furrowed even further, like she couldn't understand how that was even a thing. "Well, you can tell me all about it tomorrow. Your room is all ready for you upstairs."

"Thanks, Mom." I hugged her again. She seemed surprised at first, then relaxed into it. "I love you."

"I love you too, sweetheart," she said. "Goodnight."

"Night."

I hurried upstairs, where my room was exactly as I'd left it. The only thing different was that Mom had washed my sheets and made the bed. The walls were a light pink, leftover from when we'd painted when I was six. A blue bedspread accented the room. There was a white tree decal decorating one wall, along with a large wooden "C" above my bed. An entire bookcase was filled with my antiques collection, including everything from old thimbles to a music box I picked up at a yard sale a few years back. Pictures of my family were plastered all over the room, along with several of me and my best friend Kaylee. I wouldn't see her this weekend, since she was still traveling Europe. God, I missed her. We talked online occasionally, but she didn't get a lot of time to talk, so we barely knew what was going on in each other's lives anymore. It made me kind of sad.

I closed the door behind myself and dropped my bag onto my bed. I changed into my pajamas—the fluffy ones with cartoon sheep on them—then sat at my vanity to brush my hair into a high ponytail. As I moved through the quiet space, I couldn't get Kellan off my mind. I thought it'd be easy, until Mom mentioned the ham. Now that he'd invaded my mind, I was hopeless.

Sighing, I stood and walked over to my window. I sat on the cushioned bench beneath it and stared outside at the starry sky. Kaylee and I used to sit here and talk for hours. Sometimes, I'd lie down here and read. When Drew broke up with me, I spent hours crying into the pillows stacked against the window. Whatever it was, this bench was my place of solace, where I could relax and work through my issues.

But now, I felt stuck.

~

I woke early the next morning. When I glanced outside, frost had coated the ground, and little snow flurries were floating through the air. The sun was just barely coming up. I wasn't ready for the day—to cook Thanksgiving dinner with Mom and play board games with Dad, all while they grilled me on my classes. This semester was supposed to be the best four months of my life. Instead, it'd turned out to be the most frustrating I'd experienced yet. I didn't know if Kellan and I were supposed to stick this out or go our separate ways, and that frustrated me more than anything else.

I showered and dressed, then headed downstairs. I found Dad in the kitchen sneaking a piece of pumpkin pie. He jumped when he heard me and whirled around, shoving the plate behind himself on the counter. His mouth was full, and he had an innocent look on his face, like he was a kid who'd been caught with their hand in the cookie jar.

"Cora." He relaxed. "It's just you."

"Is Mom on your case about saving it for dinner?" I asked.

"What can I say?" he said. "Your Mom's a great cook."

I crossed the room to the fridge and opened it, then pulled out the pie tin on top. "I won't tell if you won't tell."

A smile crept across Dad's face, then he hurried to get me a plate and a fork. We sat at the kitchen table and ate our pumpkin pie together.

"Hey, Dad," I said when I was halfway through. "Do you mind if I borrow the car?"

"For what?" he asked.

"Nothing really," I said honestly. "I just want to drive around town. I miss it."

"You know your Mom wants your help cooking this morning, right?"

I nodded. "I won't be long."

Dad sighed, then reached into his pocket for his keys. "Fine, but be back in an hour."

"Thanks, Dad." I took the keys and headed to the front door to grab my shoes and jacket.

Eagle Valley wasn't very big, so it didn't take a long time to drive around. Still, I was surprised at how much had changed since I'd been gone. There was a new bookstore next to the restaurant on Main Street, and the bank had moved to a new location. The antique store I loved so much had expanded, but they were closed this weekend, so I didn't get a chance to go in. I drove by Kaylee's house, as if hoping to spot her car—like she might've come home from Europe to surprise me or something. But she wasn't there.

Eventually, I found myself at the edge of town, parked across the street from the Galen High Mansion. It was all red brick and endless corridors, with trees surrounding the property. The street was completely deserted, and every-thing was so silent it almost seemed unreal. The snow had picked up from earlier, dusting the high peaks of the mansion with little flurries. It seemed picturesque. I just sat there in the car, looking up at the mansion. I wanted to go inside and visit Grace's tomb. She was one of the Originals, a child of the higher gods. It seemed like finding direction when nothing else made sense started with turning to your ancestors for answers.

But I knew she wouldn't have them. She was gone—her essence returned to the earth and now a part of the rest of us.

I didn't know what I was doing when I stepped out of the car. I put my hood up and walked across the vast lawn to the front doors of the school. I tried to open them, but they were locked. No surprise there.

Still, I felt a pull to the school I couldn't explain. It was like it held the answers—as it did throughout my entire high school experience. Maybe I was just being nostalgic. Or maybe I was a little insane. Either way, I didn't want to leave.

I started walking around the side of the school, like I might find a window cracked open or something in this chilly weather. But all the windows were locked tight, as were the back doors. My feet continued to carry me into the woods behind the school, down a long, narrow path I'd become accustomed to over the years. After several minutes of walking, the trees opened up to a wide, grassy clearing that sloped downward at a steep angle. It was our training site for flying and elemental essence when I went to school here.

I stepped out of the trees and took in a deep breath as my eyes scanned the deep valley. It was cold out, but not so cold that it was unpleasant. The light snow muffled any other sounds, and a single ray of sunshine shone down into the valley. It was beautiful and so, so peaceful. I felt the urge to fly around like I had so many times here.

Why the hell not?

I stripped off my jacket and set it on the ground, then pulled my t-shirt over my head until I was standing in only my tank top. The cool air brushed across my skin, sending goosebumps all over my arms. But I didn't care. I just wanted to fly.

I flexed my shoulders, and my wings grew out of my back. I spread them out wide, then took a running start and leapt off the ground and into the sky. My stomach somersaulted in my abdomen, and my heart beat in exhilaration. I spread my arms out to the side and closed my eyes, letting my wings carry me slowly to the ground. I felt so free as I soared around the secluded valley.

I got close enough to the bottom of the valley that I could land, but I decided not to. Braving the cold winds, I flapped my wings and shot upward into the sky. I raced to one end of the valley, and then to the other, performing flips and aerial tricks as I went. After several rounds, I began feeling the strain, so I started my descent to the ground again. When I reached the snow-coated grass below, I fell onto my back with my wings stretched out at my sides. I expected the air to be cold down here, but it wasn't. It was actually kind of pleasant.

I looked up to the clouded sky to watch the snowflakes gently fall toward me. I was surprised at how good it felt to just sit here out in the winter weather, as if I didn't have a care in the world. I didn't know how long I lay there, just thinking things over.

Maybe I'd just stay here and not go back to school. It was easier. If I went back to school, I'd have to deal with

Kellan again, and he was impossible. He couldn't seem to make up his mind. One second he was joking with me and we were laughing, and the next he was making some back-handed comment or *blaming* me for an accident. What did he even mean that I constantly proved him wrong? That was some next-level emotional manipulation or something. Did he not realize how hard I'd worked these past few years to get into Harris Academy? Did he not see how much I'd been studying this semester to make it through our finals? Did he not notice the effort I put in to make our team better? Did he not realize that I actually *cared*?

No, probably not. Because he didn't care. I didn't know why, but it just didn't seem like any of this mattered to him as much as it did to me. He was probably only there to get with Celina anyway. Freaking perfect, show-off Celina.

Oh my God. What was wrong with me? I was being obsessive. I was—

"Cora."

A male voice sounded from directly above me. My eyes shot open, and I was surprised to see my dad staring down at me. He nudged my leg with his foot. He breathed a sigh of relief when I moved.

"Are you alive?" he joked.

I groaned and pushed myself to a sitting position. I suddenly realized how cold it was and wrapped my wings around myself. "Yeah, I'm alive. What are you doing here?"

Dad held my coat out to me. He must've retrieved it from the top of the valley before he ventured down here. I pulled my wings in and slipped my arms into the warm jacket.

"It's been over an hour," he said. "I called your phone, but you didn't answer. Your mother and I were worried."

"Oh, sorry." I reached into my jacket pocket and pulled out my phone. The screen read three missed calls. "I lost track of time."

Dad must've caught my low tone, because he suddenly looked concerned. "Are you okay?"

I didn't look up at him. I just shrugged and said, "I'm fine. It's just…"

Dad didn't care that the ground was wet and cold. He saw that his little girl needed him, and he plopped down on the ground next to me and wrapped a warm arm around my shoulder. A lump rose to my throat as I leaned against him.

"What's wrong?" Dad asked in concern. "You can tell me anything. You know that, right?"

I nodded, but I didn't answer right away. Finally, I found my voice. "I've just been dreaming about the academy my entire life. I've never wanted anything more than to become a firefighter and a healer. And I wanted to be great, but…"

Dad didn't prod. He was nice like that. He let me come to him at my own pace. Tension wrapped around my head, and a burning sensation stung my eyes.

"It's not what I dreamed it would be," I admitted.

It pained me to say. How could the academy be anything less than I dreamed? I didn't think I wanted to admit it to myself until now. I wanted everything to work out with Kellan and me because if it didn't, it meant that on some level I had failed. It meant that the academy wasn't the dream I'd always pictured it to be. Even now, the words didn't feel right on my tongue.

Dad squeezed me tight to his chest as I blinked the tears away. "I understand, Cora. Sometimes reality isn't as great as our dreams."

"It isn't," I agreed. "Not even close."

"Do you want to tell me about it?" he asked.

I pulled away from him and ran my hands over my face. "My partner and I don't get along well. We haven't all semester. It feels like we've just been going through the motions so we can pass, but that we aren't making any real strides. And when I thought we were starting to get along, he decided that he doesn't want to keep working with me."

Dad frowned, looking concerned. "I'm so sorry, Cora. I know this is what you've always wanted."

That was an understatement. It was more than just *want*. It was a passion, a desire that had consumed me to my very core since I was a kid.

"Tell me about your partner," Dad encouraged. "Why is it that you don't think you two get along?"

I shrugged. I wasn't sure how much I could tell Dad. He'd think I was making a big deal over nothing. But it *was* a big deal. Not just because the academy mattered to me, but because *Kellan* mattered to me.

Oh, shit!

It hit me like a ton of bricks. Why hadn't that occurred to me before? How could I be sitting here thinking Kellan's comments hurt because all I wanted was the best shot at my academic career? Chancellor Harris had already promised a reassignment if we wanted it.

But that was just the thing. I *didn't* want it. I wanted Kellan on my team, because even though we had our differences, and even though we didn't always get along, we had some damn good successes. We had the potential for so much more—and in more ways than one. So, where was the problem?

"Do you want to know why your mother and I get along so well?" Dad asked.

I knew Dad was only trying to make sense of the things I didn't want to say aloud, but I decided to humor him anyway. "Because you were made for each other?"

Dad chuckled, then said, "No. It's because we put the work into our relationship. There are two things that are the key to holding our relationship together. The first is communication."

"Yeah, because you two disagree all the time," I said sarcastically.

"It's true," he argued. "We do. But we also *listen*. We hear each other out, until we understand where the other person is coming from. And when we do that, we almost always find that we're on the same page and just translating our feelings into different terms."

I carefully considered his words. Lack of communication was definitely one of mine and Kellan's downfalls. He barely talked about himself, and when I tried to get him to, he shut down.

"What's the second key?" I asked.

Dad looked me straight in the eye and gave me a single-word answer. "Trust."

I waited for him to say more, but that was it. "Trust? Isn't that kind of a given?"

"Is it?" Dad asked challengingly.

Silence settled between us for a few moments. Snowflakes continued to fall, lightly dusting our clothing. "So, you think that's my problem? Communication and trust?"

Dad shrugged. "I don't know what your problem is. I was just talking about me and your mother."

I knew Dad sensed what was going on more than he let on, but I didn't push it. He'd given me something to think about.

"Any other words of wisdom?" I asked. I was half joking, but I kind of wanted more anyway—anything to help.

Dad thought about it for a moment, then said, "You need to treat each other as equals. That said, before you can work together, you have to learn to work with yourself."

I scoffed. "That makes no sense, Dad. They're two completely different things. Besides, I could never heal on my own."

"I didn't say you had to heal alone." Dad pressed a finger to my chest. "Good teamwork comes from the heart— when you're confident in yourself and no longer in competition with your teammates."

I am not in competition with Kellan, I wanted to say, but I bit my tongue. It would only result in some sort of lecture from Dad that I wasn't actually listening to what he was saying.

"Here, Cora." Dad leaned over and picked up a couple of sticks that had blown from the trees in the last storm. They were thicker than my thumb and longer than my forearm. He handed one to me. "Break this."

I eyed him curiously, but I took the stick anyway. "Why?"

"Just do it," he encouraged.

"Okay..." I took the stick in both hands and easily snapped it in half.

From beside me, Dad snapped the other. He looked back to me proudly. "See? We're each strong enough to break these sticks on our own. Now break them together."

He took one half of my stick and one half of his and handed the two of them to me in one hand. I didn't know where he was going with this, but I was intrigued, so I followed his instruction. I tried to snap the sticks together, but it wasn't as easy as snapping the first. I even pressed them against my leg to get them to give way, but no matter what I tried, I couldn't get them to break.

"I can't," I told him, handing them back.

He shook his head and pushed them back into my hands. But instead of making me try again, he placed his hands beside mine, his fingers curled around the sticks. "Do you trust me?"

"Yes, of course." What kind of a question was that?

"We'll do this together, then," he stated. "On three? One... Two... Three."

Dad and I tightened our hold on the sticks and twisted. A satisfying *snap* sounded, and the sticks broke in two. I smiled proudly.

"Some challenges are too big for a single person," Dad said. "But before we can break the sticks together, we must know how to break them on our own. Get it?"

I nodded as I let his words sink in.

Communication. Trust. Find myself.

It couldn't be that easy, not after Kellan and I spent an entire semester back and forth trying to make this thing go.

But maybe it *was* that easy…

I looked up into my father's blue eyes. "Thank you, Dad. You've been a big help."

"Have I?" he sounded shocked, but I could sense it was for show.

My lips twitched at the corners. "Yeah. We should probably get home and help Mom with the cooking."

"Good idea," he said. "She's probably worried sick."

Dad and I stood and headed back to the parking lot. I followed behind him as we drove home in separate vehicles. When we arrived home, Dad stopped me on the porch steps.

"Cora, there's one more thing I think you need to hear." Dad sounded serious.

"What?" I asked, trying to keep an open mind.

He took a deep breath. "Essence isn't the only thing we leave behind when we go. We also leave our legacy, our mark on the world. And no matter how big or how small that mark is, it's still there. The gods who created us are long gone, and we have no one to answer to. All we have left are basic human values, and we must adhere to them—not because there's something for us after this life, but because there isn't. This is your one and only shot, Cora. What will you leave behind?"

My mouth hung agape. It wasn't a question I thought I could answer. Months ago, I would've said my purpose was to heal, but after talking to Dad today, that seemed so superficial.

Dad turned to the door and stepped inside, leaving the question hanging. And it was in that moment that I finally realized what I had to do.

$\mathcal{I}$ took a deep breath as I entered the Activities Center Sunday night. I hoped Kellan would make it. I'd sent him a text hours ago, and he still hadn't responded. Typical.

It was dark out, and the campus was quiet, since most people didn't want to venture out in the snow. But I'd brave any weather to see Kellan again. Things were about to change, and I had to prove to him the academy didn't make a mistake putting us together.

The Activities Center hallways were eerily silent. The only sound I heard was the beat of my own footsteps against the tile. When I got to Gym B, I was pleased to see that the lights were on, inviting me inside. No one was around.

I dropped my gym bag at the foot of the bleachers and stripped my coat off, shoving it inside the bag. I sat down and opened my phone—waiting...

I expected to see a response from Kellan by now, but I

didn't. While I waited, I scrolled through my phone, but that didn't help calm me. I tapped my foot and watched the door as the minutes ticked by. It seemed like an hour, but I'd only been there ten minutes.

I was so full of energy that I couldn't stand to just sit. So I stood and let my feet carry me to the starting platform. Dad's words echoed in my mind, his lesson resonating louder than a bass drum pounding against the side of my skull. Kellan and I had to work together—truly *together*, as pieces of a whole. But to do that, I had to know where I stood first—where my strengths and weaknesses lied, so that he could fill in the missing parts.

I placed my foot on the balance beam and spread my wings out to the side to keep myself steady. I began inching my way across the beam, wobbling as I went. I was almost to the other side when I lost my footing and nearly fell into the foam pit, but I spun my arms and flapped my wings to regain my balance. My heart was pounding at the near-failure, but I straightened up and crossed to the other side. I breathed a sigh of relief when I was once again standing on a solid platform.

The monkey bars were next. I used the same strategy I had the last time by grabbing on to the outside support bar instead of the rotating spokes in the middle. I made it to the other side with ease, then started on the ropes. The swinging steps were just as easy.

When I reached the incline wall, I paused at the bottom. This was the task I couldn't complete on my own last time —the first in the course that required teamwork... But Kellan had reached the top of the wall himself.

Because Kellan is taller and stronger than you, I thought to myself. I didn't feel bad about it. It just was what it was. Kellan had used his strengths to get us up that wall, and this was one area where he was stronger than me.

I already knew we could conquer this obstacle together, so I skipped over it and walked around to the next platform. We hadn't gotten this far before, so I had to study these tasks to come up with solutions to get the two of us through them.

The sixth obstacle had a small trampoline at the base of the platform, with a large, rotating spoke hanging above the pit. It looked like a steering wheel on a car, only parallel to the ground and much bigger. A platform had been placed in the middle of the pit. When I'd watched the other teams, I saw that the platform was on some sort of track that made it move when you landed on it. If you didn't push the platform back once you made it to the other side, your partner had no hope of completing the task.

I eyed the moving platform, calculating my aim. After taking a deep breath, I leapt onto the trampoline, then sprang upward. My hands curled around the metal spoke, and my body's momentum sent me swirling in an arc. I let go before I made a complete rotation and landed firmly on the platform beyond. It moved easily beneath my weight, shooting down its track and slamming against the side of the stationary platform at the end. I bent my knees to stay steady. Finally, everything became still, and I stepped off onto solid ground.

Looking back toward the rotating spoke, I tried to

calculate how hard I'd have to push the platform to get it in the right position for my teammate to land on it. I thought I had it down, but the platform moved easier than I anticipated. It bounced off the stoppers at the end of the track, then started back in my direction. When it stopped, it was several feet away from me, but too far away from the spoke. I couldn't reach it to try again. Had we been competing against other teams, we'd have failed.

But we weren't, so it didn't really matter. I just had to try again until I got it down.

Walking around the side of the course, I came up beside the platform and pushed it to the end, where I tried again to get it back to where my teammate would need it. I tried four more times. Each time, I pushed either too hard or too soft, and it never ended up in the right location.

Finally, I got it to stop right where I aimed. I tested it twice more until I was sure I had it down, then moved on to the next obstacle.

This one was the one that was made of two panes of glass set parallel to each other. Celina and Rhys had climbed across going back-to-back. As I paced around to look at it from every angle, I realized that strategy was probably the smartest idea, but I still wanted to figure out if there was a better solution.

I stood on the platform between the two walls and placed my hands on one side and legs on the other, wedging my body between the two large panes of glass with my belly pointed at the ground. I was thrilled to see it was working, but it was hella hard to keep myself upright. I was a little shocked at the core strength it took to accomplish.

Though my limbs shook, I began to inch myself across the pit. Every movement I made was calculated so I wouldn't slip. But I was taking too long, and my body was getting tired. I moved my foot to the right—and that was it.

My whole body went tumbling down into the foam pit. I landed on my front and rolled over, but that only sent me sinking further into the pile of foam cubes. I tried to find my footing, but it was like the pit was endless. I only sank in further.

A male voice chuckled from above me, and my gaze darted in the direction of the sound. My heart flipped wildly in my chest when I saw Kellan's blue eyes staring down at me from the platform above. He looked thoroughly entertained.

My whole body went still as I drank him in. He looked even better than the last time I'd seen him. He wore a white t-shirt that stretched tight across his muscled chest, with a blue zip-up hoodie over the top. His legs were exposed beneath black athletic shorts. Could a guy's calves be considered sexy? Because Kellan's definitely were. And then there was the blond hair falling into his eyes, the dimples, and the slight smirk I no longer wanted to slap off his face. In fact, there were other things—much better things—I'd like to do to his lips.

"How long have you been watching?" I asked, though I didn't take the harsh tone with him I normally used.

"Long enough." He leaned down and held out a hand. "Need help?"

I felt like I should reply with a snide comment or something—since that was the usual dynamic between the two of us, but I hesitated.

"Yeah, thanks," I said instead.

I took Kellan's hand, and my whole body came alive. Butterflies danced around in my stomach, and my mind raced with what I would say to him. Luckily, he spoke before I did.

"So, what are we doing here?" Kellan asked once I'd crawled out of the pit and was standing beside him. He crossed his arms, like he was still in defense mode. I didn't blame him. I'd be mad too if someone broke my wing—no matter the circumstances.

I gestured around at the gym. "To finish the course!"

Kellan looked confused at my chipper mood.

I sighed, then plopped down on the foam platform, with my feet hanging off the edge into the pit. I patted the spot beside myself and said, "Sit."

Kellan pressed his lips together, looking skeptical.

I raised an eyebrow at him. "I don't bite."

He hesitated, then sat beside me. We were so close that we'd be touching if I leaned over only an inch.

"I'm not sure I believe that," he said.

"Okay," I caved. "I don't bite *hard*."

I playfully snapped my teeth at him. He rolled his eyes.

Silence settled a moment later, and I knew we could both sense things were about to get serious. Kellan turned his gaze down into the pit and swung his legs, lightly kicking at the end of a foam cube. He took his sweatshirt off and set it beside himself, perhaps just for something to do with his hands.

I took a deep breath before I dove in. "Look, Kellan. I know you want to quit working with me when the semester's over, but whether you like it or not, we're a team until our final. Please give me another chance. I know we can do amazing things—together."

Kellan raised his gaze to mine, giving me a shell-shocked expression. I suddenly felt self-conscious. I could feel myself turning red.

"What?" I asked, pushing my hair out of my face.

"You said *we*," he pointed out.

"Well, yeah," I said. "Because we're a team."

"But you never call us *we*."

I furrowed my brow. "What do you mean?"

"It's always *me*. *I* healed. *I* put out that fire. It's like, one of your Cora-isms."

My eyebrows shot up. Did I actually talk that way?

Instead, I said, "Cora-isms? Is that a thing?"

"It is now," he said. "This is the reason we're no good together. You're always trying to do things on your own, like with the obstacle course. But I'm not here as your side-kick, Cora. I'm here as your equal, your partner."

I opened my mouth to say something, but he continued before I could get a word in.

"The only reason you work with me is because you're forced to."

"I could say the same thing about you," I reminded him.

He shrugged, like he couldn't argue. "The thing is, if you

didn't need an Aedes to heal, you'd be on your own. That's no way to live, Cora."

Every time he said my name, it was like warm, smooth honey washing over my skin. I loved hearing the sound of my name on his lips.

"I know all that now, Kellan," I said. "But please don't pretend like you were perfect."

"I know I'm not," he said quickly. "Far from it. But I already knew it wouldn't work from the start."

"So you didn't even try?" I asked.

Kellan frowned, and I could see the guilt on his face. "You're right. I didn't try."

"I want to try," I said. "We still have two weeks until the final. I can't make up for breaking your wing—which I'm so, *so* sorry about. But maybe I can make up for the rest of it. I'm sorry about everything. I want to work together now."

Kellan stared down at me, like he was trying to figure me out. I just sat there staring back to let him know I wasn't messing around. The whole time, my heart beat wildly. I feared he was going to shut me down.

"Okay," he finally said.

I breathed a sigh of relief.

Kellan rose to his feet. "Show me what you've got, Cora. Let's beat this course."

I beamed as I followed Kellan to the starting point. He stripped his white t-shirt off, and I had to tear my gaze away so I wouldn't stare.

"Okay, Team Captain," I said. "You take the lead."

"Me?" He sounded shocked.

"Yeah," I said with a shrug. "I trust you."

Kellan cracked a smile. "In that case, ladies first."

"Ooh," I joked. "Such a gentleman."

He pressed the button to start the timer, then gestured me forward. I stepped onto the balance beam, and he placed one foot on the other end to steady it. I barely had to use my wings to balance. When I reached the other side, I did as he had and placed my foot on the beam so he could cross.

I stood in front of the next obstacle, ready to jump and grasp the bars, but instead Kellan said, "Up you go."

Before I knew what was happening, his hands were grasping my hips. I was too stunned to question it, so I just went along with it. I jumped, and Kellan hoisted me upward effortlessly, like a cheerleader. I climbed on top of the bars, feeling steady even over top of the rotating spokes. I turned back and held my hand out for Kellan, then helped him up with me.

"This was smart," I said as we crawled across.

"It's best to conserve our energy for the end," he said.

"See?" I replied. "Look what happens when we work together."

I jumped down on the other side, and Kellan quickly followed.

"Go ahead," he said when we reached the ropes.

I grabbed for the first one then swung across to the next. I didn't hesitate, or the rope might not have had enough swing left in it to get back to him. I finished the ropes, then glanced back to see he was close behind.

The swing steps were easy. I couldn't recall a time when

Kellan and I moved together in such synchrony. It felt different… and intense.

Next came the wall Kellan had fallen off last time. He ran ahead of me and got to the platform on the first try, then held his hand down to help me up. He shot me a glance when I got to my feet at the top.

"Don't worry," I assured him. "I have no plans to throw you off this time."

"Throw me off?" He raised a teasing eyebrow. "Is that what you did the first time?"

"Do you really think I'd do that?"

Kellan shrugged, but I could see the hint of a smile tugging at the corner of his lips. "Dunno."

"Well, you better get going before I do it again," I teased.

Kellan nudged me. "Stand back."

I did, and beautiful black wings sprouted from his back. He leapt from the platform and soared down to the next one. I stared after him, practically drooling at the sight of his wings spread out in all their glory. It was even hotter than his exposed chest.

Kellan landed, and his wings disappeared. "Well, are you coming?"

Oh, shit. He'd caught me staring.

I quickly flexed my shoulders and spread my wings, joining him on the ground.

"I saw you practicing this one, so I think you should go first," Kellan said.

"Okay." I retracted my wings and stepped up to the trampoline, then did as I practiced before. I went swinging around the spoke, then flung myself to the moving platform. When I reached the other side, I pushed the platform back to Kellan. I held my breath, hoping I'd given it just the right amount of force. It bounced off the other end of the track a little, but only came back a few inches. Kellan could still make it.

"Come on!" I cheered for him, clapping my hands together. "You can do this!"

He glanced up to the rotating spoke and looked as if he was calculating his jump. He gave the trampoline a few test jumps to see what kind of force it had. Then he backed up and took a running start. His hands curled around the spoke, and his legs flew in an arch, before he let go and swung onto the platform. It shifted under his weight and sent him gliding over to me.

"Woohoo!" I cried. "We did it."

Kellan looked like he was getting tired, but so was I. "We're not done yet, sweetheart."

My heart lurched at the term of endearment. He didn't mean it in *that* way, did he?

"Come on," Kellan said, like he hadn't just called me sweetheart. He kicked his sweatshirt aside that was still sitting there from when he took it off before. We stood back-to-back and hooked our arms together like Celina and Rhys had done during Grand Opening. I was acutely aware of Kellan's bare skin pressing against my shoulders.

"Press against me as hard as you can," he said. "Don't hold back, okay? We need to create as much tension as we can."

"Okay. I can do that," I agreed.

We each placed one foot on the walls in front of us, then I felt him press his back tightly against mine. I pushed my leg hard against the wall, until we were locked tight enough that we could both get our other foot up without falling over.

"This is a good start," I said.

"Yep," Kellan agreed. "We have to keep this kind of tension the whole time. Understand?"

"Yes," I answered.

"Okay. One foot at a time."

"Got it."

Kellan and I started inching across the obstacle. It took a lot of strength to stay pressed up against him, but I pushed through it.

"Almost there," Kellan said.

My knees were wobbling, but I forced them to steady and continued moving along with his rhythm. I stared forward, trying not to focus on the pit beneath me. Before I knew it, I caught sight of the end of the wall in my peripheral vision. I glanced down to see we were already over the finishing platform.

"Down on three?" Kellan asked.

"One, two, three," I counted.

We stepped down at the same time, but I lost my balance and stumbled into him. Kellan caught me before I face-planted into the pit. His hands were warm on mine—comforting. What I wouldn't give to have him touch me in other ways...

Kellan straightened and cleared his throat. "One more

obstacle to go."

"Right." I nodded, then turned to the final obstacle.

It was a giant rope net that climbed to a high platform above us. After all the energy we'd put into the last few obstacles, it looked like an impossible feat. My legs groaned beneath me, and my arms felt like noodles. But I wasn't about to give up now, not when we were so close.

I looked up to Kellan. "Together?"

He gave a firm nod. "Together."

We raced to the net and began climbing, keeping pace with each other as we went. The net was incredibly wobbly, which made it even harder to climb than it looked. But I kept moving forward, pushing as hard as I could without worrying about how far away the finish line was.

Kellan and I reached the top at the same time. We climbed onto the platform, both breathing heavily. He reached out and helped me to my feet. Together, we stumbled toward the buzzers at the end.

My hand hovered above mine as I glanced to him. He did the same.

"Ready?" he asked.

"Ready," I confirmed.

We pressed the buttons at the same time, and the scoreboard let out a loud *buzz*. I sighed in relief and plopped onto my butt, trying to catch my breath. I expected Kellan to be out of energy, too, but he wasn't. He walked to the end of the platform and shot his fists into the air.

"Woohoo!" he cried toward the direction of the bleachers. "That's right, bitches! We did it!"

I chuckled. "There's no one out there, you weirdo."

"Well, there should be," he replied. He hammered his fists against his chest like a gorilla, then let out another loud *whoop!* Wings shot out of his back, and he jumped off the platform, gliding down into the foam pit between the glass walls.

"Oh my God, Kellan," I said between laughs. "Calm down. It's only an obstacle course."

Kellan pulled his wings in and twisted in the air. He landed on his back in the pit, sinking deep into it. He looked up at me and said, "Get down here, Cora."

I rolled my eyes, but I couldn't resist. I spread my wings wide and soared down to him. I did as he had done and pulled my wings into me, then twisted in the air and landed in the foam pit beside him. I giggled as the rush overcame me.

The two of us were still trying to catch our breath as we stared up at the gymnasium ceiling.

Kellan was the first to break the silence. "You look freezing."

I glanced over to him to see he was eyeing my arms, which had broken out in goosebumps. "No, just cooling off."

He wouldn't take that for an answer. He rolled onto his stomach and crawled through the foam pit to the edge, where his sweatshirt was lying. He grabbed it and tossed it over to me. "Here, take this."

I was about to protest, but then his scent hit me. I couldn't even describe what it was like. It smelled like a warm embrace—if that made any sense. All I wanted to do was wrap the sweatshirt around me and never take it off.

"Thanks," I said sheepishly as I slipped my arms into it.

It was soft and smelled like Kellan. This guy didn't know what he'd just done.

He plopped onto his back again beside me. I lowered myself to my back until our heads were almost touching. I could feel the heat coming off of him, and it made my whole body quiver. I wanted to move closer—to touch him —but I didn't.

"Kellan," I finally said when my breathing slowed.

"Yeah?" he asked.

"I think I know why we've had such a hard time this semester."

"Oh?

"I don't think we understand each other," I admitted.

He chuckled. "That's the understatement of the year."

"No, I'm serious." I kept my eyes on the ceiling while I spoke. It seemed easier to talk without looking him in the eyes. "I hardly know anything about you."

"What do you mean?" He nudged me with his elbow, and my breath caught in my chest. "You call me an asshole all the time."

I smirked. "That's because you are."

"See? That's all you need to know."

"I don't know what you think about me." I held my breath, awaiting his response. The truth was, Kellan had told me more than once what he thought about me, but I couldn't help but wonder if things had changed. They had for me. "Why'd you hate me so much when we were paired up?"

He took a long breath, like he was contemplating the

question. "It was that whole icebreaker thing," he admitted. "You kept blaming everyone else and wouldn't take responsibility. You didn't trust anyone."

I blinked a few times, absorbing his words. Had I really been that much of a bitch?

"And then there was the whole *Davina power* comment," he said.

"Oh, come on," I defended. "I was just… you know."

"No, I don't know," he replied. "The Aedes and Davina are equals, and you kept acting like the Davina were better."

I frowned. "I never meant to. I'm sorry."

Kellan sighed. "The truth is, I never wanted to come to the academy anyway."

"Wait. What?" I finally lifted my head to look at him. I knew I'd said before he acted like he didn't want to be here, but it was different hearing him admit it.

Kellan didn't even look at me. "I'm only here because my dad wanted me here. He wanted me to become a healer like him, but I've always wanted to be a lawyer."

I suddenly remembered the law book I'd seen in his dorm room. I should've realized.

"Why do you want to be a lawyer?" I asked.

He finally tore his gaze from the ceiling and turned to look at me. "Remember how I told you my mom is human?"

I nodded. "Yeah, how does that even work when we can't tell humans what we are?"

"The Alliance put laws in place to keep us from revealing ourselves to humans," Kellan explained. "In special circumstances, however, they make exceptions. My parents fell in love, but before my dad could tell her the truth, he had to undergo an application process, interviews, and get a license so they could make sure she wouldn't tell anyone. Then once he told her, *she* was rigorously interviewed, and honestly, the secret itself was a lot to swallow. She almost left my dad for keeping it from her."

I gasped. I couldn't imagine.

Kellan took a deep breath. "Anyway, Mom says it would've been a lot easier if there was a bigger support network in place for mixed families and that the laws were a little more lenient so you didn't have to go through such a long process just to share your secret with someone you love. Mom never felt like part of our world, even though she married into it."

With every word Kellan spoke, my heart sank for his family. His mom obviously really mattered to him. I could tell there was more to the story than he was saying, but I didn't prod.

"You want to change all that," I guessed.

He nodded. "I want to create a program for mixed families, a way to educate and support the spouses and children. My ultimate goal is to get voted into the Alliance and work with them to make better laws."

"I think that sounds great, Kellan," I said honestly.

"Anyway," he continued. "My dad and I agreed that I'd spend one semester at the academy, and if I didn't like it, he'd pay for the rest of my schooling. Do you know how expensive law school is? I couldn't exactly say no."

"So… what'd you decide?" I was scared to ask. "Do you like the academy, or are you giving it up for law school?"

Every muscle in my body froze as I awaited his response. My chest twisted into knots. I wanted him to stay with me, but I feared he wouldn't.

"Wait, Kellan." I stopped him before he could open his mouth.

I shocked the both of us when I rolled over and threw my arms over his chest, pulling him into an embrace. It should've been awkward, since we were sinking further and further into the foam pit and it wasn't much of an embrace anyway. But we were touching, and it felt right.

"Before you say anything, let me say something first," I said into his shoulder.

Kellan relaxed and rested a hand on my back. Oh, God. Something about that gesture was everything I needed. It was like he was accepting me.

I drew away and stared into his eyes. They would've made my knees go weak if I were standing up. I spit the words out before I could stop myself. "Kellan, at the beginning of the semester, I hated you as much as you hated me. But… something changed. I don't know what it was. Maybe it was when you saved me from those protestors. But whatever it was, you showed me that you weren't the guy I thought you were. I know I tell you you're a jerk all the time, but it's not true. You're actually kind of nice, and you can be sweet sometimes."

His expression remained blank the entire time. I had no clue what he was thinking, but I pushed on. If I hesitated, I'd never finish what I had to say.

"I stuck with you, but it turned out to be better than I imagined. I don't want to lose you. I want to stay on your team. If that means working harder, then I'll take it. But…"

Kellan's expression finally shifted to curiosity. "But…?"

I swallowed down the lump in my throat. I couldn't sit here and guilt him into staying on my team just because I felt something for him. It wouldn't be fair. I knew what Dad had been trying to tell me now with his last bit of advice. My parents' legacy wasn't the sealing of the realms and the breaking of the Aedes' curse. Their legacy was in the kindness they showed and the differences they embraced—and they'd shown me that through every step of my life. They supported me in everything I did. And I wanted to pass on the same legacy, which meant I had to do the same for Kellan now—no matter what he decided.

"But," I said, "I'll support you in whatever you want to do."

Kellan took a deep breath, then started to get up. I drew away from him and sat up in the pit, until we were facing each other. My hands quivered. I couldn't believe I'd just said all that to him. I was dying to hear his response.

"I'm glad you feel that way, Cora," he finally said. "Because there's something I need to tell you."

My blood ran cold. Yeah, I was wearing this wonderful warm sweater that smelled like Kellan, and my blood ran cold. Whatever he had to say didn't sound good.

He glanced down to his hands and started picking at his fingernails in his lap. Yep. Definitely not good.

"I'm not coming back next semester," he spat out.

My heart sped up a little, but I couldn't say it wasn't

what I expected to hear. It wasn't what I *hoped*, but I wasn't surprised. "Then that's what you have to do," I told him, trying to be the supportive partner I said I'd be.

He shook his head, still refusing to meet my gaze. "There's more. Over break, a friend of my dad's called me up and said he'll be in town in two weeks. He's the president of Dunmar University."

"Oh my God," I said. "That school's super prestigious."

He nodded. "I know. And they have the best pre-law program in the country. He's invited me to dinner. If I go, it could secure my entire future—the university, the pre-law program, and everything after that."

"Then you have to go," I encouraged, even though my stomach felt empty and that knot in my chest kept tightening.

"The thing is, Cora..." Kellan hesitated, and I instantly knew there was more. "He's only in town on the night of our final."

I recoiled. It felt like he'd just slapped me across the face. "Wait. Hold on. Are you saying you're *ditching* our final?"

Tears began to well in my eyes. This was way worse than leaving at the end of the semester. This was a complete betrayal of our partnership! If I didn't pass this final, I could flunk out. He was gambling my dream away at a chance to get his!

"Cora..." He reached for me, but I instantly backed away.

I glared at him, unable to truly wrap my head around what he'd just told me. "I thought part of being partners was that we trusted each other," I snarled, blinking away the tears.

"Cora, I'm sorry," he insisted. "But this is my future."

"And this is mine!" I exploded.

I was so angry that when I opened my mouth, I couldn't get any words out. I thought I could support him, but this went beyond any decision I thought he'd ever make.

I couldn't even look at him right now. I started toward the edge of the pit, but it wasn't the dramatic exit I was hoping for. My arms and feet sank into the pieces of foam, and I moved at a snail's pace. I probably looked like an idiot, but I didn't care. I had to get out of here.

"Cora, wait," Kellan called.

I reached solid ground and whirled toward him. Unlike me, he moved through the foam with ease. He reached the platform and pulled himself up before I could get a word out.

And now I was a freaking mess, so I couldn't talk anyway. Tears streamed down my cheeks, and I wiped them away with the sleeve of Kellan's sweatshirt.

"I—I thought—" I sobbed.

"I'll talk to Chancellor Harris," he promised.

"What good is that going to do?" I snapped, still wiping at my eyes. "I can't go through the final without a partner. I'm going to flunk out."

My chest heaved, and uncontrollable sobs bubbled up in my throat. I was so embarrassed.

"Cora, they're not going to flunk you because I—" he started, but I quickly cut him off.

"This academy is all about teamwork, Kellan," I

snapped. "They grade you based on how your team performs. So yeah, if you're not there, I can pretty much guarantee I'll fail."

"Cora—"

I didn't want to hear any more. If Kellan had stuck this out until the end of the semester and *then* decided to leave, I could've lived with that. I would've even thrown him a going away party or some shit like that. But this…

I whirled around and stomped toward the bleachers to grab my bag, then headed for the door, fuming. It was just my luck that Celina decided to step into the gym at that exact moment. Her eyes met Kellan's first from where he stood dumbstruck on the obstacle course.

"Hey, babe!" she called over to him. "I've been looking everywhere for—"

She cut off when she noticed me approaching, a hard expression fixed to my face. I didn't mean to, but I was so mad I barely noticed where I was going. I slammed my shoulder into hers on the way out.

"Hey!" she cried. "What's your problem?"

I whirled toward her, my breath hot. "You wanted him to stay at the academy with you? Maybe *you* can convince him. Because I sure as hell can't."

Celina's gaze darted to Kellan. He was already making his way toward us from across the gym.

"Kellan, what's she talking about?" Celina asked.

Part of me was glad he hadn't told her. It was the one ray of sunshine on this whole matter. But I couldn't bring myself to rub it in. I turned and started down the halls toward the doors. He called for me, but I ignored it.

As the sound of my name echoed down the halls, one thing became very clear. Kellan Greene didn't want this life —the healing, the firefighting, any of it. But I had enough determination and resolve for the both of us.

With or without him, I was passing that exam.

Even though it was late, I marched straight to the Academy Center and to Chancellor Harris's office. It was a long shot that she'd be here at the end of a holiday weekend, but I had to at least check. The reception desk was empty, but her office door was open a crack. I stepped toward it and knocked.

"Come in."

My heart skipped a beat when I heard Chancellor Harris's voice behind the door. I pushed it open, and she glanced up to me from where she sat at her desk. Her lights were off, but her computer glowed brightly.

"Cora," Chancellor Harris said lightly. "What can I do for you?"

I stepped further into the room. Anger continued to course through my body, but it was more than that—it was disappointment. I tried not to let any of that show.

Instead, I found myself saying, "You're still here."

She gave a slight smile and said, "Yes, I'm known to overwork myself a little. Please, have a seat."

I sat in the chair across from her. My lips tightened, and my jaw tensed. "Chancellor Harris, I'm here to petition to complete my final exam on my own—without a partner."

Her brow furrowed, and she tilted her head to the side a little. "Why would you want to do that?"

An image of Kellan's face flashed through my mind, and my hands tightened in my lap. "My partner's bailed on me."

Chancellor Harris frowned. "Your final exam requires a group effort, Miss Marek."

"I know," I said. "But what happens if I don't go through with it?"

She took a deep breath. "You'd fail out of the academy."

"I can't let that happen," I stated. "This has been my dream since I was a kid."

"Perhaps I can talk to Mister Greene," she offered.

"It doesn't matter," I replied. "He doesn't care if he flunks out, and he's already made plans for the night of the exam."

Chancellor Harris looked speechless, like she wanted to help but didn't know what options to give me. "I'm sorry that you were put into this situation, Miss Marek. I know it isn't fair. The risks are simply too high to send an individual into the exam without support."

"The risks are high regardless," I argued.

"There's a healing portion to the exam that can't be performed alone," she pressed.

I was starting to get more upset by the minute. It was

like I was being punished for Kellan's choice—and I hadn't done anything wrong. "Kellan can't be the only person on campus that I can heal with. Let one of my professors help."

"The exam doesn't just test practical skill, Miss Marek," Chancellor Harris said. "It also tests the team skills you've developed over the course of the semester."

"I was going to be reassigned anyway," I said. "Besides, it's unrealistic to expect any of us to work with the same partners the rest of our lives. People are reassigned to new locations all the time. Others die on the job and their partners have to work with someone else."

I rose to my feet, my face heating. "You and I both know I have what it takes to pass this thing. Please just give me a chance to prove myself."

I was fuming, but Chancellor Harris's expression was unreadable. I expected her to shoot back how this was the academy's policy and how they'd never had issues before. Instead, she took a deep breath and folded her hands in front of herself on the desk.

"I understand your frustrations, Cora," she said. "But no one has ever gone through this exam on their own."

I crossed my arms. "So I'll be the first."

She hesitated, then said, "Okay."

I blinked a few times. Had I heard her right? Was she really going to let me do this on my own?

"I'd like to see you pass your exam as well," she told me. "I'm willing to let you go through with it."

Excitement filled my chest. I could hardly believe she was agreeing to this.

"*But,*" she quickly added. "Should you fail the test, I can't allow you to retake it."

I swallowed the lump rising in my throat. "So I can take the test on my own, but I can't ever reapply for the program if I fail?"

She nodded. It was better than skipping out on the test altogether and flunking out. At least this gave me a chance.

"And I'll still be reassigned next semester?" I asked. "No repeating my classes?"

Chancellor Harris nodded. "Provided you pass."

"I will," I stated confidently. Inside, I was giddy with excitement. "Thank you so much for this opportunity."

"You're welcome, Miss Marek," Chancellor Harris said as I started for the door. "Good luck on your exam."

I only hoped that the second chance she'd given me was enough to get me to pass.

Two weeks later, I stood in front of the burning building questioning everything I'd gone through this semester. The sky was dark, in stark contrast to the bright orange flames and white snow on the ground. The heat came in waves across my face like a warning, like I shouldn't be going into this test alone. But this was my future we were talking about. If I didn't do this, I'd never become the EMT I'd always dreamed of being.

"Are you okay?" Laura asked from beside me. She'd come for emotional support, since she wasn't in the fire-fighting program and already took her earth final yesterday.

I nodded, but inside, I was screaming.

We stood on the corner of an intersection across the street from a burning house. It was a controlled fire, one that the school had been hired to start as part of a demolition project. It doubled as the perfect location for our final exam. I knew I wasn't in any real danger, since my professors would be keeping close watch, and we each had an alarm attached to our uniform, but it was nerve-racking nonetheless.

All along the block, people had come to watch the fire. Some were students and faculty here to support their students. Others were nearby residents who couldn't resist checking things out. Down the street, the protestors that called themselves the Infantry walked with picket signs. I hadn't seen them around campus since the incident, but this was new turf for them to play on. I could see that Colt douche from here. He was yelling obscene things into the crowd so fiercely that his face had turned beet red. Campus security was doing their best to keep the protestors far away from the fire.

Close by, Celina and Rhys were staring up at the fire, looking like they'd already won the challenge. Caleb and Shaylene were on the other side of the lawn, going through their dressing drill.

I'd already completed the drill and wore my heavy fire-fighting gear—helmet, jacket, gloves, and all. I even wore a pair of steel-toe boots that I'd secretly slipped my Davina Blade into for good luck. My breathing apparatus cylinder was attached to my back, and I held my mask in my hand. Even though I could control fire, my essence wasn't enough to protect me. There was still a chance of falling debris, unexpected flames, and poisonous gas. The gear provided an extra layer of protection should something get out of hand. Just thinking about it made my guts twist.

Laura stepped in front of me to look me in the eyes. She took me by the shoulders. "Before you go in there, Cora, I want you to know how incredibly proud I am of you. Kellan never deserved to be your partner. You have the determination and the skill to do whatever it takes to get through this. It's time to show Kellan how wrong he was about you. You can do this. Make me proud."

I forced a smile. "Thanks. I will."

Laura didn't take her hands off me. Instead, she drew my essence into herself, and I felt my channel opening, the essence buzzing through my body. It was enough to power me up for the night.

"I'll be here when you're finished," Laura said, dropping her hands. "Then afterward maybe we can get a bite to eat to celebrate."

"Celebrate what?" I asked.

"Your test, of course!" she said. "Because you're going to pass. I know it."

I felt her confidence wash over me. "Yeah, I am."

"You are what?" Travis asked as he came up to us. Caleb and Shaylene were at his side in their gear.

"She's going to pass," Laura said brightly.

Travis draped an arm over her shoulder and gave her a light kiss. "Good. We want you around next semester, don't we?"

"Absolutely," Shaylene agreed. "I still can't believe you're doing this on your own, though."

"What choice do I have?" I asked. "Chancellor Harris said I'd flunk out if I didn't go through with this."

"Don't worry," Caleb said. "I'd do the same thing. You'll do great."

Shaylene stepped toward me and slipped her arm into

mine. "You should stick close with us. After all, in a real scenario, there'd be multiple teams going in at once."

"Are you saying this isn't a real scenario?" Travis balked, pointing to the burning building in front of us.

"Fair enough," Shaylene said.

Caleb looked deep in thought. "I don't know if it'll work for her to follow us. Each team gets a different route."

Shaylene's shoulders fell. "Right."

"Guys, I'll be fine," I assured them. "Laura powered me up for this part, and I've got Professor Sanders waiting on the other side to power me up for healing."

"That's the spirit!" Laura encouraged.

"Okay, everyone!" Professor Kovski called. She stepped up to the middle of the lawn with a clipboard in her hands. "All firefighting students, please gather around."

I waved to Travis and Laura, then followed Caleb and Shaylene to stand beside our classmates.

"This is a three-part test," Professor Kovski explained. "It simulates a real-life situation using the key lessons you've learned in your classes over the past four months. This test will prepare you for the next three semesters. If you cannot complete the tasks, you will not be deemed a fit for the remainder of the firefighting and EMT courses at Harris Academy."

She continued. "In this mock scenario, the house caught fire when a burning candle was knocked into the curtains. The parents escaped, but their six children are still trapped inside. Your first task is to follow your route—which I'll provide you with in a moment—and retrieve the dummy in the room marked on your map. You will rescue them following the safety procedures you've learned in your firefighting class."

She pointed to a group of ambulances parked at the curb. "Once you retrieve your dummy, your team will make its way to these ambulances, where we'll swap the dummy for lab rats and you will be tested on your healing abilities, as would be required of you in the field."

She continued. "Once you're finished there, you will join Professor Taylor and Professor Arnold at the back of the house and attempt to extinguish the flames coming from the bathroom. Any questions?"

Nobody raised their hands.

"Good," Kovski said, giving a firm nod. She reached for the papers on her clipboard and began handing them out. "Study your routes carefully. In a real-life setting, you will not be blessed with a map."

She handed me my paper, then lowered her voice just for me. "I'm sorry to hear about Kellan, Cora. Good luck in there."

I forced a smile. Just the mention of Kellan made me want to punch something. "Thanks."

She turned her attention back to the group. "Remember, should anything go wrong, we highly encourage you to use the alarms on your belt to call for help."

She held up a small red device, which we'd covered many times in class. It attached to our clothing and made a high-pitched squeal when you pressed the button.

"Your test starts now."

Kovski said it so casually that it took me a second to

realize she meant *now* now. Groups started moving, and I quickly followed behind. I slipped my mask on, which covered my entire face, then attached my regulator to it—the device that connected to the tube for my air tank, which would allow me to breathe in the fire. Finally, I added my hat, then raced inside behind the other teams. My map showed that my target was located upstairs in the second bedroom, so I immediately started toward the stairs. The entire building was up in flames, and it was nearly blinding. I was hot everywhere beneath my uniform, but my air tank made it easy to breathe.

When I reached the stairs, I was ready to do a quick assessment of the structure to see if they were safe, but Celina and Rhys were already rushing up them. I deemed it safe and climbed the stairs. In front of me, Celina was using her essence to calm the flames along the walls. I decided to save mine for the final task, since I didn't have a partner to power me up.

Celina and Rhys went into the first bedroom, and I immediately went for the second. There, I found a nursery set up, with a crib, rocking chair, and chest of drawers. I ran to the crib and found a dummy the size of an infant lying there. I wrapped the doll in its blanket and turned back to the door.

I stopped in my tracks when I saw Celina standing there. Even though her mask covered her face, I could see the anger knitted in her eyes.

"You dumb bitch!" she shouted. Her voice was a little distorted behind her mask, but I could still hear her clearly.

I was so shocked that I stumbled back a step. Was she

seriously going to do this in the middle of a burning building?

"Excuse me?" I snapped.

"You heard me," she snarled.

"Celina," Rhys called from behind her. He was carrying their dummy.

"Just hang on," she growled at him. She stepped into the bedroom, blocking my only exit.

I took a cautious step back. The murderous look in her eyes was freaking me out. "Aren't you wasting time?"

She didn't respond. Instead, she marched forward and slapped her hand as hard as she could across my face. You would've thought my mask would protect me, but it didn't. It only dug into my skin, then dislodged. I breathed a gulp of thick smoke, and my lungs burned. Primal anger pulsed through my veins.

I dropped my dummy and resituated my mask, then faced her. "What the hell is your problem?"

"You're my problem!" she shouted.

"Celina, stop," Rhys begged, tugging on her. He was so huge he could've just tossed her over his shoulder, but he didn't. "Save it for later."

She ignored him and took another step toward me until our masks were practically touching. "What did I tell you at the beginning of the semester? Kellan's quitting, and it's all your fault."

She was getting way too close for comfort, and the whole building was up in flames. The longer we stayed, the more dangerous the structure became.

"Back off!" I shoved her, and she went stumbling backward.

Her features hardened. "You don't deserve to pass this test."

"Fuck off!" I shouted. "Kellan made his choice on his own. I wanted him to stay."

"Bull shit!" she cried.

Then she lunged. Her hands went straight for my face, but I ducked, and she ended up landing on top of me. She grabbed me by the jacket and dragged me onto the ground. Suddenly, her hands were all over me. I fought back. *Hard.*

I thrust my hand outward, clipping her in the chin. Her head snapped back, and she screamed. A second later, her fist slammed down on the side of my face. Pressure shot out through my ear, and a ringing filled my head.

"Bitch!" I roared as I brought my knee up into her gut.

She grunted. A second later, Rhys was dragging her off of me.

"What the hell, Celina?" he yelled at her, trying to restrain her. "Leave it. Let's get this test over with!"

Celina elbowed Rhys in the stomach and broke free. She lunged at me again, clawing at anything she could. She ripped my hat off my head and flung it across the room, then grabbed my mask and tore that off, too. Heavy smoke assaulted my lungs and eyes. I was so pissed I could literally throw this bitch down the stairs right now.

I kicked her in the stomach as hard as I could. She went stumbling back but grabbed on to my uniform so she wouldn't fall. Even though I punched her again, she still hung on.

Rhys grabbed her around the middle and tried to drag her away from me, but she wouldn't let go. She tugged and tugged on my uniform while I tried to go the other way, but even Rhys couldn't pull her off of me.

"It's all your fault!" she shouted.

Suddenly, something on my uniform gave way. I thought I saw a chunk of something fly off, but I didn't see what it was. Celina and Rhys stumbled one way, while I went the other. I slammed into the burning wall and quickly jumped away before the flames could hurt me.

When I righted myself and turned back to Celina, she'd grabbed whatever had come off my uniform and was reaching for my dummy. "Have fun passing without this," she growled, before turning and rushing out of the room behind Rhys.

"Celina!" I shrieked, heading after her. My insides were blazing red-hot, and it had nothing to do with the fire all around me.

All I heard was her evil laughter over the sound of roaring flames. I reached the doorway and saw her stop at the top of the stairs, one arm raised. In the blink of an eye, flames burst around me with such force that I was blasted back into the room. I went reeling onto my back, but an ungodly pain shot through my skull on the way down. My head had slammed into the side of the rocking chair.

The world blurred around me as I lay there, unable to find my balance. As the burning building spun around me, I continued to inhale poisonous gas that made my airways feel as if they were on fire. I grabbed for my mask, but I could barely feel my fingers. Something warm and sticky touched the back of my head as darkness swirled around me.

Blood.

I was a fool to think I could do this alone. I reached for the alarm on my belt, but my hands couldn't find it. Was I *that* disoriented?

I was a moment from slipping into unconsciousness when I saw a figure making their way through the flames and over to me. They wore a firefighting uniform, so I couldn't make out who it was. My best guess was Celina. Had she come back to make sure I was dead or something?

Except the figure was too tall and their shoulders too broad to be Celina. The fire blazed behind him in a way that outlined his form, like he himself was glowing. He bent down to me and reached for the back of my neck to cradle my head in his arms.

"Cora," he said breathlessly.

Shock riveted through me, and I actually felt the heat melt away for a second. I turned my gaze up to his eyes through his mask, and there was no denying those beautiful blue eyes. The fall must've been worse than I thought, because there was no way this was real.

"Kellan?"

"Cora, you have to get up!" Kellan commanded.

"Kellan, I'm—" I started to say, but he already noticed. He pulled his gloved hand away from the back of my head to see it was coated in blood. He cursed under his breath.

"Kellan, what are you doing here…?" I paused to go into a coughing fit. Kellan's eyes widened, and he quickly grabbed for my mask hanging off my air tank and slipped it back over my bloody head. I breathed a greedy breath of fresh air.

"Cora, you're badly hurt," he said, ignoring my question.

I blinked a few times. My mind began to clear as the fresh air filled my lungs. "I—I can heal myself."

"Do it quickly then," he instructed.

Essence poured through me as Kellan channeled my power into him. My hand shook as I brought it to the back of my head, but I didn't give it too much thought. The more I contemplated it, the harder it would be. I felt my essence leave my hand, and a warm tingle spread across my skull, numbing the pain. My head began to clear.

"Good enough," I said quickly, pushing myself to my feet.

Kellan grabbed my arms to steady me. He glanced around the room. "Where's our dummy? We'll fail this portion if we leave without it."

"Celina took it," I told him. "What are you doing here anyway? I thought you had a dinner with some big law professor."

Kellan shook his head. "I did, but I got there and I realized—"

He was cut off by the sound of collapsing debris in the next room. His hands tightened on my arms, and we both startled.

"We can talk about it later," he said quickly. "Let's get out of here."

Kellan pushed at me, and I started for the door. By now, the stairs were completely covered in flames. I aimed my palms at them to calm the fire and get a look at their structural integrity.

"They're too far gone!" I shouted at Kellan over the groaning of the building. "The map showed a second staircase that way!"

I pointed. Kellan took my hand, and we started down the hall together. When we reached the second staircase, we saw that it was engulfed in even more flames than the last.

"I think we're going to have to take a window," Kellan said.

My heart hammered. Fire, I could deal with. Jumping out a second-story window? Not so much.

"There has to be another way," I said.

"I don't think—Look out!"

Before I knew what was happening, Kellan lunged forward and shoved me out of the way. I slammed into a door, and the wind left my chest. Debris went everywhere, kicking up smoke all around us so that I couldn't see. Then suddenly, the flames were back, burning a pile of boards and drywall that had caved in from the ceiling. Above us, a gaping hole had opened in the roof. Dark smoke billowed out of it.

All I heard were the sounds of Kellan's screams. My stomach plummeted to the floor when the smoke cleared and I saw him lying beneath the debris pile.

"Kellan!" I shrieked.

I immediately aimed my hands at the pile and killed the flames faster than I thought possible. The instant they were gone, I rushed forward and started pulling pieces off Kellan. At the same time, I used my other hand to search for the alarm on my belt, but my hand met nothing. I glanced down to see my alarm was missing.

Fuck! That must've been the thing that tore off when Celina and I were fighting.

"Relax, Kellan," I said with all the gentleness I could muster. Inside, I was a wreck. Nerves were racing through my veins, and every inch of my body was shaking. "We're going to get a rescue crew in here."

"Shit, Cora," he cried. "There's something in my leg."

I pushed enough debris out of the way to get to his

alarm, only to see that it'd been crushed under the weight of the debris.

Shit. Shit. Shit!

There was no way to alert our professors. No one was going to save us.

I quickly turned my attention to his leg. A sharp piece of metal from the roofing material had sliced through his uniform and stuck into his flesh. It was attached to a bigger piece of wood that looked almost as heavy as Kellan. Blood oozed out of the wound and dripped onto the floor.

"It's okay, Kellan," I assured him in a shaky tone. "I'm going to get you out of here."

He sucked in a sharp breath and tried to say something, but he didn't get it out.

"This is going to hurt, but if you work with me, we can get it healed and get out of here," I said.

He shook his head, but his eyes looked anything but on board with this. He looked terrified and in unimaginable pain. His face had paled, and I worried he was about to pass out.

"On three?" I said, but he just gritted his teeth and didn't respond. "One… two…"

I pushed on his leg and tore the piece of metal out before I reached three. He screamed so loud that it shook me to my very core. But we weren't out of the woods just yet. The piece of metal had caught on his uniform. I tugged on his pant leg, but it wouldn't break free.

"I can't move!" he cried, trying to roll away from the debris, but it held on to him firmly.

I pulled a second and third time, but it was determined

to hold Kellan down. The debris itself was too heavy for me to move. The best I could do was rip his pants off.

Rip his pants.

I remembered the blade in my boot and reached for it. The fire was hot on my exposed skin as I pulled my pant leg up to get to the boot. I pulled my dagger out and pressed it into the fabric. Kellan's uniform finally tore away from the debris.

"Okay, let's get you healed up so you can walk," I said as I slipped the knife back into my boot.

But when I looked back to Kellan, he wasn't moving at all. Shock had set in, and his eyes had rolled back into his skull.

"No!" I cried.

I slapped him in the chest, trying to get him to wake up, but nothing happened. A heavy weight settled on my chest, and my throat burned at the threat of tears. What was I going to do? I couldn't get to the stairs, and both our alarms were out. If we waited for our professors to come searching for us, we could be burnt to a crisp by then. The only other thing I could do was throw Kellan out the window—but who knew how much that could seriously hurt him?

Shit!

My eyes turned upward, and an idea suddenly struck me.

No… It was stupid. Beyond stupid.

I knew the consequences if I did this. I knew what people would see—and what they would say. I knew everyone in the supernatural community would judge me.

They'd all say how they'd have done it differently. But if I didn't do it, Kellan could die, and I wasn't willing to let that happen.

I stood and took a deep breath. "I'm sorry, Kellan. But it's the only way to save you."

Then I did the only thing I could. I stripped off my mask, air tank, and jacket, then flexed my shoulders. White wings grew from my back.

They say adrenaline can do crazy things to you. It's true. Kellan was heavy as hell, but somehow, I found the strength to cradle his body in my arms. I shouldn't have been able to fly with all the extra weight, but I jumped and shot out of that hole in the roof like I was a freaking superhero.

All those people on the ground—the Davina, the Aedes, and the humans—their eyes gravitated toward me like I was a divine angel sent from the heavens.

Cell phone cameras pointed my way. People screamed. I don't remember much, but I remember thinking one thing: *I don't care.*

Yeah, we had our secrets, and yeah, I got that exposing ourselves could lead to serious consequences. But Kellan was alive and free from that fire because of me. And nobody—*nobody*—could convince me that wasn't the right thing to do.

I soared over the crowd, searching for a place to land. My feet made heavy impact with the pavement next to the ambulances, and I pulled my wings into my back. The air was ice cold on my skin. Professors Kovski and Sanders raced over to me with a gurney.

"Do you have any idea what you've just done!?" Sanders yelled at me.

"Yeah," I snapped back, helping Kellan onto the gurney. "I saved my partner's life. Want to grill me about it?"

"We'll deal with that later," Professor Kovski said quickly. "Mister Greene needs immediate medical attention."

"Kellan! Kellan!" I shouted.

I quickly followed them. At the back of the ambulance, they removed his mask. He blinked a few times, and relief flooded through me. I was so happy I could cry.

Before I knew what I was doing, I flung myself over him and planted a kiss firmly on his lips. It wasn't how I planned for our first kiss to go. I didn't even realize it was going to happen until it did. My heart lifted in my chest. It felt like my first flight, my stomach somersaulting in my abdomen and my pulse tapping to the beat of a quick drum. For one split-second, the entire world stood still.

The next, it was over. Everything happened so fast that I barely felt the rush of the kiss before his hands were on my shoulders, pushing me away.

"No, Cora," he groaned.

His pained eyes met mine, and I read something in them—something that buried deep down into my heart and tore it just a little. It wasn't that he was in too much pain. He really didn't want me in that way.

I knew it shouldn't matter. There were more important things happening right now. You know, like saving his life. But the mix of sorrow and regret that entered his eyes was enough to get me to stop and slow down. And when I did that, the weight of everything that had happened tonight came crashing down on me.

I stepped away before I really decided to. It was like my feet had a mind of their own. It felt like I was floating as all sounds around me faded. Celina ran over to Kellan. I was mostly grateful, because he needed someone right now, and I couldn't handle another fight with her.

My knees were shaking so badly, and my heart pounding so fiercely, that I couldn't stay on my feet. I ended up in a secluded corner of the street and turned to the curb behind me. I sank to the ground, burying my face in my hands. Cold air brushed across my exposed skin.

Please be okay. Please be okay, I begged as they worked on Kellan.

I couldn't stop the flood of tears that rained down my cheeks as I rocked back and forth. Davina couldn't fix everything. They'd heal the wound for sure, but if something else went undiagnosed, he might experience permanent damage. I felt like a total failure—and the test wasn't even on my mind anymore. Who cared if I passed now? All I cared about was making sure Kellan was okay. And he didn't even want my help…

"Well, well, well…"

I whirled around as the sound of a sinister male voice met my ears. Colt Walter approached me through the darkness. He was alone, but there was a look in his eyes that said I should be very afraid. I shot to my feet and backed away.

"I have to say, I didn't expect that." He spoke coolly, like he was hiding some sort of secret.

"Leave me alone," I said, sounding more confident than I felt. I quickly glanced toward the ambulance, but no one was looking my way.

"There's no reason to be afraid," he sang, like he was toying with me.

"Don't you dare come any closer," I snarled in the most threatening tone I could.

To my surprise, he stopped in his tracks. "I don't want to hurt you."

"Then what do you want?" I snapped.

Colt straightened his blazer. "I want answers. I knew something was going on at this school, and this just proves it. What are you? What do your people want?"

"We just want to help," I insisted.

"Help what? Yourselves?" he accused.

"What are you talking about? No!" I cried. "Why do you hate us so much?"

"I'm not here to answer your questions," he growled, his lips curled back over his teeth like an animal.

I crossed my arms. "Then I'm not here to answer yours. Leave us alone. We aren't hurting anybody."

His nostrils flared, but he spoke in a cold tone. "Oh, but you are. And that little stunt you just pulled? It didn't go unnoticed. Soon enough, everyone will know that the people at Harris Academy aren't really people at all."

I curled my hands into fists. What was he implying? That we were aliens or something?

"We're not dangerous," I told him, but he didn't look like he wanted to hear it.

"You're not what you seem," he said, "and that means

you should be feared. And believe me, everyone will fear you. Watch out, because that can of worms you just opened can never be closed again."

"What are you suggesting?" I bit at him.

"The academy's going down," he threatened. "A war's been brewing for a long time, and now there's nothing you can do to stop it."

My blood ran cold as Colt turned on his heel and walked away from me.

A war? He couldn't be serious.

Except he didn't sound at all like he was joking.

Everyone had been right. The Aedes and Davina had kept their identity secret for a reason. Because there were people out there like Colt Walter who would stop at nothing to kill the thing they feared.

And something told me he had the means to actually do something about it.

I sat in Kellan's hospital room the next morning, waiting for him to wake. The minutes turned into an hour, but they felt like an eternity. I didn't quite feel whole, and it had nothing to do with failing my exam. It wasn't about Kellan, either. At least, I didn't think it was. I couldn't really explain it. All I knew was that my insides felt raw—empty. I'd come to the academy to make an impact on the world… and now I wasn't sure that was going to ever happen.

Celina had been here earlier, probably to gloat about winning the Chancellor's Award. I'd hid out in a corner of the waiting room until she left, then snuck inside while Kellan was sleeping. What I could gather from listening to the nurses was that the cut had been deeper than we thought and he'd lost a lot of blood. He'd recover, but he was very fatigued from it all.

I thought coming here would allow me to apologize to

Kellan about everything that had happened. I knew it wasn't my fault that the roof had collapsed on him, but I still felt like I should be sorry about something. Maybe it had to do with everyone yelling at me afterward about it. My professors, my parents when they heard… Laura seemed sympathetic—she said I'd done the right thing—but I hadn't had a chance to talk to any of my other friends yet.

Maybe that's what I was hoping for from Kellan, that he'd confirm what Laura said and tell me I did the right thing. I mean, would he rather I left him? Tossed him out the window? I did what I had to do… right?

Kellan shifted a little, and I straightened in my seat. His eyelids fluttered open, and he glanced around in confusion, like he couldn't figure out where he was. Then his eyes caught my face, and he relaxed.

"Kellan…" I said softly, not sure where to start. My body involuntarily moved toward his, but I jerked back before I could touch him. "I'm sorry."

"Sorry for what?" he asked in a strained voice. "You saved me, didn't you?"

I shook my head, though I didn't know why. I *had* saved him.

I knotted my hands in my lap. "I—I guess so, but I don't know if I did it in the right way."

"Is there a right way to save someone?" he asked. He started to sit up, but he groaned and fell back down onto the bed.

I was on my feet in an instant. "Does it hurt? What's wrong?"

"No." He waved me off. "Just stiff is all. And hella thirsty."

I grabbed the water bottle beside his bed and handed it to him. He slowly pushed himself to a sitting position.

He took a swig, then spoke in a clearer voice. "Did they freak out?"

"Did who freak out?" I asked.

"Everyone?" he asked with a raised eyebrow. "You exposed yourself last night. It's kind of a big deal."

"Oh, so you remember," I said flatly. Somehow, I had hoped he'd forgotten most of the night.

"Yeah, I remember."

"All of it?"

He didn't take his gaze off me when he spoke. "All of it."

I sat back in my chair and buried my face in my hands. "Oh, God, Kellan. I'm sorry about kissing you. It was just the heat of the moment kind of thing and…"

I wished he would've kissed me back. I wished he hadn't pushed me away. But he was right to. It wasn't fair of me to do that to him when he'd been lying on a gurney.

"Celina and I are together," he blurted, like he couldn't hold it in any longer.

My heart stalled, and I gaped at him. *Together together?*"

He nodded, his cheeks reddening a little. "When she visited me this morning, I told her that I couldn't go through with the law school thing, that I'd stay here. And so we made it official."

"But she's been stringing you along all this time!" I practically shouted. How could he have feelings for this girl? She was insane! They had no chemistry. "She tried to kill me during that test, you know."

Kellan gave me this look like he thought I was overreacting. "I talked to her. What happened was an accident."

I crossed my arms and looked away from him. How could he be on her side? "You weren't there."

"I came, though," he said softly. "That has to count for something, doesn't it?"

I turned my gaze back to him, my hands shaking. He was right. It did count.

I softened my tone. "About that… what changed your mind? Why'd you come?"

Kellan shrugged. "I got to the dinner, and everything was great, but I couldn't get you off my mind."

My heart fluttered when he said that.

"We got our food, and I couldn't eat it," he said, staring at the floor and looking deep in thought. "That's when I realized that if I truly had any integrity, I wouldn't be sitting there. I'd be at the test. With you."

He lifted his gaze to mine, and I saw a sparkle in his eyes I hadn't seen before.

"I'm glad you came," I whispered. "I couldn't have finished the test without you."

Kellan scoffed. "Well, you didn't finish it with me, either."

I cracked a smile.

"Thanks for everything you did," he said. "It's more than I could've asked of my partner."

The tension in my body melted. "Thanks, Kellan. I really needed to hear that."

A knock came at the door. We turned to see Travis's face through the glass. He was beaming and waving his hand comically at us.

"Hey, guys!" he said as he pushed the door open. Laura, Caleb, and Shaylene piled in behind him.

Laura was carrying a pile of balloons. She stepped further into the room and set them—along with a card—beside Kellan's bed. "We came to see how you were doing."

Kellan sat up straighter and set his water bottle aside. "Fine, thanks. But you guys really didn't have to come."

"Of course we did," Caleb said. "Our fellow classmate gets impaled by a piece of building. We're all here for you, bro."

Kellan offered a small smile. "Thanks."

"Have you guys been online?" Shaylene asked.

Kellan looked between the four of them. "No. I've kind of been sleeping off the whole *being impaled* thing."

"What's going on?" I asked. Concern washed over me. I didn't like the look on Shaylene's face.

"Here, I'll show you," she said.

Shaylene turned on the smart TV in Kellan's room and hooked her phone up to it. She mirrored the screen for all of us to see. As she started to scroll through social media, my stomach sank deeper and deeper in my abdomen. There were pictures and videos from all angles of me flying through the air carrying Kellan.

"You've gone viral," Travis said, like it was some sort of badge of honor.

"Viral?" I squeaked. "Guys, this isn't good. I mean, I knew people would see, but I didn't think the whole freaking *world* would see! The Alliance has strict laws about this."

Laura's face paled. "Do you think you'll get arrested?"

"Arrested?" Disbelief fell across my face. "I didn't exactly think of it as a possibility until now."

"You should see what they're saying about you," Travis said, like it was cool. "An angel sent from the heavens. Archangel Michael himself."

"Archangels are only stories based off the Originals," I said. "They were never real."

Travis shrugged. "Yeah, but *they* don't know that."

"Besides, do I really look like a *man?*" I rolled my eyes, but it was only to lighten the mood. Inside, my mind was running zig-zags. I knew what I was getting into when I flew Kellan through that roof, but I thought I'd get a slap on the wrist for showing myself to a few people. The videos Shaylene was casting on the screen showed millions of views.

"Calm down, Cora," Kellan said, keeping the level head he always did. "The Alliance will understand you were trying to save me. They've dealt with this stuff before. It'll be old news by this afternoon."

His reassuring tone helped calm me.

"I hope so," I said.

A second knock came at the door, and we all turned to see Chancellor Harris stepping into the room. We all exchanged a quick glance, but no one seemed to be able to explain what she was doing here.

"Hello," she said, nodding toward each of us. Her tone wasn't as bright as usual, which made my mouth go dry.

She'd probably come to drag me away to the Alliance or something.

Caleb cleared his throat. "Um, you're probably here to talk to Kellan. We'll give you some space."

I stood to follow my friends out the door, but Chancellor Harris stopped me. "Sit, Cora. I'm here to speak with you, too."

I ducked my head and returned to my seat, waving to my friends as they left the room. When the door shut, silence fell between the three of us. Uneasiness twisted in my gut. Chancellor Harris stood at the end of Kellan's bed in a black pantsuit looking super prim and proper. Her expression was hard to read, but I sensed it couldn't be anything good.

"You're coming back to the academy," she stated, like it was mere fact.

"Wait… what?" I couldn't be sure I heard her right.

"What do you mean?" Kellan asked at the same time. He shot me a quick, confused glance. "But we failed. If you fail your exam, you're dropped from the program."

Chancellor Harris took a deep breath. "I need you two close… So I can protect you."

Kellan and I shared another glance.

"Protect us from what?" I asked.

She frowned. "The Alliance isn't pleased with what happened last night. They'll find a way to cover this up, but I'm sensing that won't be enough. Things have been changing these last few years, and it's only a matter of time before all hell breaks loose."

"All hell breaks…" I could hardly process what she was

saying. So Colt had been right. A war was coming. "But we help people!"

She shook her head. "Sometimes, that is not enough."

"Why do you want to help us?" I asked.

"The academy will be under close watch given the location of the incident," she said. "If anyone comes after you two, they come after the academy. And I can't let that happen. This world needs us."

Kellan's confusion dropped from his face. He held his head a little higher and said, "You're damn right they do. We'll help any way we can."

It hit me instantly that Kellan had said *we*—as in, we were a team. Like he took responsibility for what happened as much as I did. And when he turned his gaze to mine, I saw it in the way he looked at me.

In that moment, one thing became very clear. Kellan maybe didn't like me in *that* way, the way he liked Celina, but I was important to him in another. We were partners— for good.

I was touched. I couldn't explain it, but that emptiness inside of me seemed to fill when I saw that look in his eyes.

I turned to Chancellor Harris. "So what are we going to do?"

Chancellor Harris took a long breath. "The only thing we can do, Cora. Prepare for what's coming."

END OF BOOK ONE

Continue the series in book two of the Divine Descendants Duology, *Exposing Magic*.

ABOUT THE AUTHOR

Alicia Rades is a USA Today bestselling author of young adult and new adult paranormal fiction. When she's not dreaming up magical stories, she's either binge-watching paranormal TV shows, meditating, or spending time with her family. She has an unhealthy obsession with psychic characters and writes with a deck of tarot cards next to her computer.